"But I wanted you to make love to me, Ty."

He was silent, watching her, conflicting expressions crossing tense features. The sigh came from deep down. "Ria, don't get me wrong. It isn't that I didn't feel anything. You crawled under my skin that first morning. But you're still young in a lot of ways—and a romantic."

"I'm no younger than I was when we made love."

"Ria, we're not talking about the same thing. You need looking after. You don't belong out here. Listen to what I'm saying—I don't want to get involved. Do you understand?"

"Yes." Ria felt wretched, her chest aching. The time had gone so fast. Two weeks ago she hadn't even known what wanting a man was like. Now she knew too well.

KAY THORPE, an English author, has always been able to spin a good yarn. In fact, her teachers said she was the best storyteller in the school—particulary with excuses for being late! Kay then explored a few unsatisfactory career paths before giving rein to her imagination and hitting the jackpot with her first romance novel. After a roundabout route, she'd found her niche at last. The author is married with one son.

Books by Kay Thorpe

Don't miss any of our special offers. Write to us at the following address for information on our newest releases.

Harlequin Reader Service
901 Fuhrmann Blvd., P.O. Box 1397, Buffalo, NY 14240
Canadian address: P.O. Box 603,
Fort Erie, Ont. L2A 5X3

KAY THORPE

jungle island

Harlequin Books

TORONTO • NEW YORK • LONDON
AMSTERDAM • PARIS • SYDNEY • HAMBURG
STOCKHOLM • ATHENS • TOKYO • MILAN

Harlequin Presents first edition April 1987
ISBN 0-373-10973-3

Original hardcover edition published in 1986
by Mills & Boon Limited

CHAPTER ONE

DIMLY lit and smoke-hazed, the bar was crowded. Men only, so far as Ria could see from where she hesitated in the doorway. Not the kind of place women would frequent by choice, she supposed. Sleazy was the word which sprang most readily to mind.

The Singapore waterfront was no place for any female, period, she was bound to admit. Wasn't that the very reason she was playing down her own femininity? Not that she had ever made much of it at the best of times. Girls had few advantages so far as she was concerned.

Morgan, the man had said. She should have asked for a few more details perhaps. Judging by the looks of some of these characters, she would be better advised to steer clear of the whole idea—except that she would then be back at square one again. The cheapest passage available cost more than she was prepared to squander. Find the man first, then make judgment.

The barman nearest that end of the long counter was Chinese. He eyed her inscrutably as she approached.

'I'm looking for a Captain Morgan,' Ria said, dropping her voice a tone to lend credence to the illusion she was endeavouring to create. 'I was told I'd find him in here.'

'Over there,' said the man in English, flicking a thumb in the direction of a booth where four men sat playing cards. 'You want dlink?'

Ria shook her head. 'Not right now.'

Half deafened by the sheer volume of noise issuing from several dozen male throats, she threaded her way through the knot of men between bar and booth. The card-players were cocooned within a small pool of light cast by an overhead shade pulled down low over the

5

table. None of them took the slightest notice of the denim-clad figure which halted on the perimeter of their group. Of the four, two were dark-haired men in their thirties, answering to the general description she had received; the other pair could be discounted due to age and colouring.

'See you,' said the one with his back to her to the man directly across from him. He watched the cards laid face up on the table, giving vent to a groan as the message went home. 'Damn you, Ty! I could have sworn you were bluffing!'

'*You* had to be,' returned the other, raking in the pot without visible self-satisfaction. 'Want another game?'

'Is one of you called Morgan?' asked Ria before anybody could answer, thankful for the protecting shadow of the peaked cap when they all looked up.

'I'm Morgan,' acknowledged the man with the cash. His voice was deep-timbred, accents clipped. Accentuated by the overhead light, his face seemed all planes and angles, the skin taut and deeply tanned. 'Who wants to know?'

'I'm told you're leaving for Brunei in the morning,' she said, ignoring the question for the moment. 'I'm looking for a passage.'

'I don't carry passengers,' he came back, transferring his attention to the deck of cards again.

'I'm willing to work it,' countered Ria gruffly. 'For nothing more than my keep.'

The older man said something low-toned, drawing a coarse laugh from his immediate neighbour. Morgan allowed himself a faint downward tilt of a lip, viewing her slight build in the denim trousers and loose jacket, the youthful curve of jawline, the wide spacing of dark blue eyes.

'I don't need another deckhand,' he responded. 'If I did I wouldn't be taking on some kid too young to shave! Cut on out of it, sonny. Try again when your voice finishes breaking.'

'I'm no kid!' Ria protested with some heat. 'And I'm stronger than I look.'

'You'd need to be.' He was already dealing the cards. 'It's still no.'

Ria stood her ground, chin jutting determinedly. 'All right, if you won't take me on, do you know of anyone else going to Brunei in the next couple of days?'

'If I did,' he said on a note of impatience, 'I wouldn't be pointing you in that direction. Go back home, wherever that is, before you run into trouble.'

'Thanks for nothing!' Ria turned on her heel and moved blindly away from the table, recognising the futility in further appeal. She heard the laughter following her, and knew her cheeks were burning. It had been a long shot, though one she had felt bound at least to try. Travelling to Borneo as a fare-paying passenger was going to make serious inroads into her reserves, but she was left with little choice. Even if she could find some other ship going in the right direction it was likely that she would meet with the same response.

The 'kid' rankled most. At twenty she had been further and done more than many twice her age. Last year there had been the Overlanders tour to Katmandu, and before that a dozen different ventures, including the stiff Outward Bound course which had gained her the coveted gold medal. Given the time she could have found a cheaper and far more interesting way of getting here to Singapore than flying, only it was already mid-August and the monsoon was due in October. By then she hoped to be back home with her task fulfilled.

It was hotter outside than in, the night air oppressively still. Ria made her way down the wharf, eyeing the vessels moored there with resignation growing by the minute. There was no telling where any of them might be going, and she could hardly climb aboard each one to ask. Like it or not, she was going to have to settle for a berth on the *Malindi* sailing the day after tomorrow. That meant two more nights in some back-street hotel, but it couldn't be helped. Her father

would have appreciated her problem. In following his
last wishes she felt closer to him now than at any time
when he had been alive. Not that there had been much
opportunity for closeness these past years. His work
had filled his life to the exclusion of almost everything
else.

Brought up by an aunt from the age of five when her
mother had died, Ria had lived for the rare occasions
when her. father was between expeditions and able to
afford her a little attention. An anthropologist of some
repute, he had often been away for months at a time,
with little or no correspondence to ease their passage.
From an early age, Ria had been convinced in her own
mind that had she been born a boy things would have
been different. She had made every effort to prove
herself as good as any boy on the physical side, at least,
excelling at sport, always ready for any challenge.
Pretty dresses, parties, all the things beloved of her own
sex were without interest to her. She had captained an
all girls' soccer team, played cricket for her local side on
more than one occasion, had reached blue belt standard
in judo and was a county standard swimmer. It was
only in the past year that she had come to realise she
might have stood a better chance of impressing her
father by following in his academic footsteps, only by
then it had been too late.

His death from cancer at the age of forty-eight had
not been an easy one. Ria had nursed him through the
final days herself. At first she had believed his
'confession' to be hallucination brought on by the drugs
he was taking, but he had assured her it was the truth.
While in Borneo five years previously it appeared he
had met and actually married a woman from a tribe he
called the Ukits, and had a son by her. He had left the
two of them there in the jungle village when Western
civilisation had beckoned him home, but the guilt still
lingered. With almost his last breath he had asked Ria
to find the woman, who was named Jemo, and make
sure she and the boy were provided for.

Which would have been relatively simple, Ria thought now, had there been unlimited funds, only that had not been the case. After everything had been settled she was left with little more than nineteen hundred pounds, and five hundred of that had already gone on a return ticket out here. The rest, changed only that afternoon into Malaysian dollars, was tucked into a special pocket stitched inside the waist of her jeans. Dangerous to carry so much so far, she knew, but better than hanging around waiting for transfers to be effected. The way things were going she would be lucky to finish up with a round thousand by the time she reached her destination. Long Laha was several days' journey up the Rajang and Balui rivers. That would also have to be paid for, unless she could persuade someone to take her for free. And she still had to get back here to Singapore in order to utilise her ticket home. All in all, she might have been better advised to book straight through to Brunei in the first place instead of trying to save to a few pounds this way.

What she would do when she did eventually get back to England she hadn't yet stopped to consider. There was always the dole queue if nothing else turned up. Neither her aunt nor anyone else in the family knew her real purpose in making this journey. They wouldn't be likely to understand. Ria had found it difficult enough herself in the beginning, despite her father's protestations that the native population of Borneo no longer consisted of ignorant savages. Jemo had been educated in Belaga down-river. Along with many others, she spoke excellent English. She had also, he had added wistfully, been very beautiful, both in feature and in disposition. She had saved his life after a wound sustained on one of his jungle treks had become infected. For many months he had been content to live the Ukit way of life while continuing his studies of the various tribes. It was only when home began to exert its pull again that he had finally acknowledged the sheer impossibility of the situation. He had left in the night, abandoning mother and child to their fate.

Someone was following her along the wharf. Ria melted into the shadows between two warehouses, drawing a breath of relief when she saw the lone man weaving an unsteady path in her wake. A drunken sailor returning to his ship, that was all. He probably hadn't even seen her. There was no one else around. The whole wharf appeared devoid of life.

Watching the man, she saw him stumble over a rope left carelessly uncoiled and disappear from sight down behind a stack of crates waiting for dispersal. He seemed to be a long time getting up again. After several minutes had elapsed. Ria made a hesitant approach. If he was hurt she could hardly go and leave him lying there, drunk or not.

She found him sitting up with his head clasped between his hands, elbows propped on bent knees. There was blood on his fingers—at least she assumed that was what the dark stain was. He lifted a blank gaze when she spoke to him, eyes unfocused.

'Gotta get up,' he mumbled. 'Gotta get back.' He was speaking more to himself than to her, attempting to stir unwilling limbs into action. 'Just one li'l drink tha's all!'

Just one little drink too many, by the sound of it, reflected Ria drily. There was a cut on his temple, she could see that now, though she doubted if he was feeling much pain from it. He needed help of some kind, that was certain. Left to his own devices he might even pass out. He had to be at least fifty, she assessed; what hair he had left was streaked with grey. His condition aside, he looked decent enough.

'Let me give you a hand,' she offered, hitching the canvas duffel-bag more securely on to her shoulder. 'If you can get on your feet you can lean on me till we get to that ship of yours.'

He made no protest as she assisted him to a shaky stance. Scarcely three inches taller than her own five feet six, he was of a wiry build that carried few excess pounds. Ria bade him sling an arm about her shoulders, supporting him about the waist. This close, the smell of whisky was strong enough to make her wrinkle her nostrils.

They went down to where the smaller craft were berthed at the end of the wharf. The one to which Ria's charge eventually managed to direct his footsteps was built along the lines of a trawler, with the bridge housing admidships and a covered hold aft of the main hatch. Getting the man down the iron ladder to the deck several feet below proved an onerous task. Ria was immensely relieved to achieve it with no more than a grazed wrist for her pains. There seemed to be no one else on board. At any rate, no one came to discover what all the noise was about.

Below decks was spick and span and unexpectedly spacious. The main saloon had banquette seating along both outer bulkheads, plus a dining area fronting the narrow galley. A closed door for'ard gave the impression that one or two sleeping cabins might lie beyond.

'S'll do,' groaned her companion, sinking gratefully down on the nearest of the cushioned seats. 'Gotta sleep!'

He was out almost before the words had left his mouth, snoring like a grampus in happy oblivion. The cut on his head had stopped bleeding and looked superficial enough to have little bearing on his condition. Probably better to leave it alone, Ria considered. He might suffer a headache when he eventually came round, but he would have done that anyway.

There was an atmosphere about this boat that appealed to her, although if her erstwhile companion was an example of the crew, it was surprising to find things so well ordered. Having a look round while she was here surely wouldn't hurt. If anyone caught her at it she could always explain the circumstances.

As she had imagined, the for'ard door gave access to a narrow alley off which lay two compact cabins, each containing a couple of pull-down bunks. A short companionway led up to the bridge itself, the latter lit by the wharf lights. Ria studied the various instruments and laid a tentative hand on the polished brass wheel-spokes. Her only real experience of boats was under sail during the Outward Bound course, yet somehow she felt quite at home. This craft might not be over large, but she would bet it could take just about anything the sea could throw at it.

There was a chart table to the rear, with a roll of parchment laid ready across it. Ria opened the latter out of sheer curiosity, feeling her breath suddenly dry in her throat as she looked at the faint lines pencilled in, the notations made. Singapore to Brunei, there was no mistake about that. Talk about the blind leading the blind! The question was when?

Not the only question, came the deflating realisation. Finding another boat going where she wanted to go was only half the battle. All the same, it would be something of a start to know the sailing date. There was no indication that she could see on the chart itself.

The man below in the saloon was still snoring. He came only half awake when Ria shook his shoulder, peevishly protesting.

'When are you leaving for Brunei?' she asked urgently, willing him to respond. 'Brunei! Do you understand?'

'Mornin',' he murmured, burrowing deeper into the cushions in an effort to escape back into his stupor. 'Get lost, Mike. Just wanna sleep it off, tha's all!'

Mike. A nice ordinary name, anyway. Doubtful if he was the captain though, considering the term of address. She stood there a moment chewing thoughtfully on her lip. If she waited until the crew returned there was no guarantee that passage would be provided, whereas if she simply found somewhere to hide until they were well out to sea there was probably little chance of time being wasted in turning round to set her back on shore. Stowing away aboard a craft manned by unknowns was a risk, she knew, but it was a calculated one. Standards of housekeeping on board ship reflected character pretty accurately according to all she had been taught. Whoever he was, the captain of this particular vessel had to be man of some integrity.

It was now almost ten o'clock. To be reasonably safe, she would need to allow at least twelve hours before she made her presence known. A further excursion for'ard revealed a couple of large storage lockers tucked under the bows of the ship. One was fairly well stacked with various items of gear, but the other allowed plenty of room for either sitting or lying. There was even a deflated rubber dinghy she could spread out as a bed. Which just left the problem of sustenance. Food she could manage without, hungry though she was already feeling, water was something else again.

A search of the galley turned up an empty plastic bottle which seemed clean enough. Nevertheless, Ria took the precaution of rinsing it out throughly before filling it with fresh water from the tank. Finding an open tin of biscuits in one of the lockers, she helped herself to a handful. Eked out one at a time, they would help stave off the pangs of hunger through the long night to come. By now she was thoroughly into the whole idea, refusing to think any further ahead than the immediate problems. The toilet was almost opposite the locker she had selected, which would be of considerable, if somewhat risky, advantage if the need became desperate enough. She could hope to sleep most of the night after all she had gone through this last couple of days.

The man stretched out in the saloon had stopped snoring and was beginning to show some signs of returning consciousness. If she was going to do this thing at all the time had better be now, before the rest of the crew turned up. Taking a last glance around to satisfy herself that all was as she had found it, she switched off the single light she had used and made her way for'ard again.

With the locker door closed, space was limited but
not impossibly so. At least there was plenty of air
getting in, hot though it might be. Taking off the denim
jacket and cap, Ria made herself as comfortable as she
could on the layer of rubber and tried to compose her
mind. There was no point in dwelling on what might
happen in the morning when she finally made her
presence known. Getting through the night was enough
to be going on with.

The heat became stickier as the minutes ticked away.
She could feel the perspiration springing from every pore.
The rubber beneath her wasn't helping, she realised. She
would be better off on the bare boards in the long run.

Opening the door a little in order to gain room to
move, she froze at the sound of footsteps on the deck
overhead, the sudden burst of masculine laughter. They
were coming back!

Somehow she managed to gather the deflated dinghy
and shove it into a corner, pulling the door almost
closed again and listening at the crack. She heard a
voice raised suddenly and wrathfully, although the
exact words were indistinguishable, and felt a pang of
sympathy for the man most likely to be on the receiving
end of the tirade. Not that he hadn't asked for it,
getting himself into that state. It was even possible that
he had been the one supposedly left on watch. The one
thing she hoped was that he would have no recollection
of being helped back on board by anyone, or suspicions
might just be aroused. Even the most cursory glance
would be bound to expose her.

Peace fell again, broken only by the muted sounds of
the harbour. After fifteen minutes had passed she felt
tension begin to ease. So far so good. What she needed
now was sleep. She had experienced worse conditions
than these in Nepal last year. She was warm, she was
dry, she had good solid boards beneath her and food
and water to hand. What more could anyone ask?

*   *   *

The ship was in motion when she awoke. Not the gentle rocking that might be associated with harbour waters, but the full rise and fall of open sea.

Sitting up as far as she was able, Ria stretched cramped limbs, stifling a groan as the blood began to flow again through the arm on which she had been lying. She felt both sticky and grimy, but at least it was cooler. That in itself had to be a bonus.

The illuminated fingers of her man-size watch stood at seven-thirty. Allowing for the time that had passed to her knowledge before she had finally dozed off, she must have slept for at least seven hours. That couldn't be bad, even if she didn't feel too much benefit from it right now. She was on her way. That had to be the most important thing.

There were two biscuits and a little of the water left. The latter was warm, but it wet her lips. She dampened a tissue and rubbed it over her face and hands, then ran her fingers through the boyish crop of fair hair before re-donning the blue cap. No point in putting on her jacket again until she was ready to go out and face the music. Cooler than last night though it might be, it was still pretty stifling down here.

Keeping up the deception for several days on a ship this size might be difficult anyhow, she acknowledged. While her figure wasn't exactly voluptuous, it did have certain feminine attributes which could only be disguised up to a point. One shock at a time had to be her aim. Let them get used to having her aboard first, then spring the rest. She could handle any situation that might possibly arise from her change of sex. Self-defence was her speciality.

Apart from the throbbing of the engine and the slap of waves against the hull, no sound penetrated her cubby-hole. The captain, and perhaps his first mate, would be up on the bridge, the other members of the crew about their various tasks. This far for'ard she would be unlikely to hear anything, unless someone came to use the toilet. The bridge was the best place for

confrontation. It was likely to be an uncomfortable few
minutes; she was hardly going to be welcomed with
open arms. Still, it had to be gone through. Staying
hidden away down here for several days was obviously
out of the question.

She stuck it out for another two hours just to be sure.
With the jacket securely buttoned and her cap pulled
well down over her eyes, she pushed open the door and
crawled out into the alleyway. Her legs felt unsteady
when she gained her feet. She leaned against the near
bulkhead for a moment or two until she recovered full
use. Somebody shouted something up on deck,
seemingly right above her head, which was answered
faintly from the stern end of the ship. Ria pushed
herself resolutely upright and started along the alley
towards the bridge companionway. The sooner she got
this over with the better.

The sudden opening of the door leading through to
the saloon just as she reached the bottom of the
steps took her by surprise. Judging from his expression, the sight of her standing there took the man who
came through the door by shock. Brief though Ria's
glimpse had been the previous night in the bar, there
was no mistaking that mane of reddish hair. Her mind
already racing ahead to draw the probable and heart-
sinking conclusion, she could only gaze at him
mutely, waiting for the inevitable. She should have
realised, of course. The coincidence alone should have
warned her.

Recognition was mutual, that was immediately
apparent. 'I'll be damned!' came the soft ejaculation,
followed by a grin that was as encouraging as it was
unexpected. 'Don't give up easy, do you, kid? Hope
you're a good swimmer!' He didn't wait for any answer,
coming forward to mount the first couple of rungs and
push open the hatch. 'Hey, skipper, we've got a
stowaway aboard!'

There was an audible curse from above, the tone of it
causing Ria to wince involuntarily. Watching her, her

captor grinned again with a certain relish. 'He didn't even get started yet. You're going to wish you'd steered well clear by the time he's through with you, kid, take my word!'

'Stop jawing and get him up here,' came the clipped command. 'Sharpish!'

Responding to the jerk of a thumb, Ria slung the duffel-bag more securely over her shoulder and moved to obey the injunction, pulling herself easily up the rungs. The bridge was bathed in sunlight, the brasses gleaming. The man standing at the wheel gave her a swift, comprehensive glance as she straightened, his expression unnerving.

'When did you come aboard?' he demanded.

'Last night,' she said gruffly, refusing to cower. 'About ten.'

She wouldn't have thought it possible for that iron-hard jawline to tauten still further, but she was wrong.

'Get Jack,' he commanded the man at her back.

Jack had to be the drunk left in charge, Ria surmised. She wondered how much he would remember. She made no attempt to speak as steely grey eyes turned her way again. The question of whether or not she would have done what she had if she'd known whose ship this was was surperfluous now. She was here. Nothing she could say or do was going to alter this man's way of looking at things.

'Cat got your tongue?' he asked after a moment. 'You'd plenty to say for yourself last night.'

Ria shrugged, not trusting her voice. It was going to get worse than this. Far worse. Wait till he found out who and what she really was! For a wild moment she wondered if it might just be possible to keep her secret after all, but common sense soon put paid to that idea. She could hardly keep on the disguising jacket and cap over three or four days. Best to face that particular problem when she had to. Right now she had enough to be going on with.

The anger in him was well under control; that in itself

was a comfort of sorts. She stole a glance at him from beneath lowered brows as he turned his attention back to the instruments in front of him for a moment. Tall and lean-hipped in the shabby denim jeans, he had shoulders like an ox, the muscular structure of his back and upper arms shown to full advantage by the sleeveless white vest. The cap pushed to the back of his dark head was the sole concession to his status.

'How old are you?' he rapped without taking his eyes from the view ahead.

'Twenty,' she said, and heard him snort.

'Like hell! More like sixteen. Where do you come from?'

There was no point in fabrication. 'England,' she told him.

'I meant now—recently.'

'Two days is recent, isn't it?'

'Don't get clever,' he warned. 'I want the truth.'

'It *is* the truth.' She was still addressing the broad back. 'I flew in on Tuesday.'

The breath hissed suddenly and impatiently between his teeth. 'You're asking for a rope end across your butt!'

'It wouldn't alter facts,' Ria came back tartly, momentarily forgetting her role. 'Why don't you try asking me something useful, like the reason I need to get to Borneo in the first place?'

The dark head swung her way, a sudden odd expression in the grey eyes as he surveyed her. Ria faced up to the scrutiny with a defiant tilt of her chin. If he'd guessed he'd guessed. It had to come some time. It would be a relief to have the whole thing out in the open.

Whatever he might have been about to say was lost as the outer door opened again to admit her companion from the night before. He was looking a lot fitter than the last time she had seen him, the strip of sticking plaster across his temple the only obvious reminder of his former state. A frown creased his weathered forehead as he looked at Ria. There was even a flicker of recognition in his eyes.

'Never saw him in my life before,' he blustered. 'How'd you get on board, son?'

'Walked,' supplied his superior grimly. 'While you were flat on your back. And don't try telling me he couldn't have got past you. A whole army could have come aboard for all you'd have known about it!'

'Yeah.' The older man looked sheepish and uncomfortable. 'I guess you're right at that. That knock on the head must have put me right out.'

'Plus the whisky.' There was the briefest pause before the other added softly, 'You didn't leave the ship at all, I suppose?'

'Who, me?' There was indignation in the denial. 'A drink's one thing, but since when did I ever . . .'

'O.K., O.K.' Ty Morgan sounded resigned. 'Let's leave it right there. She's running a bit rough. Take a look, will you?'

'Sure.' The little man was unreservedly eager to be on his way. 'Right away, skipper!'

At least there appeared to be no intention of putting about, thought Ria with cautious optimism. Hurdle number one passed.

The red-headed crew member came back on the bridge as Jack left it. He was shorter than the captain by an inch or two, Ria noted, and of somewhat finer build in his striped cotton T-shirt. 'You're too easy on him,' he stated flatly. 'It isn't the first time, it sure as hell won't be the last!'

'Maybe.' The other's tone was non-committal. 'He isn't the problem right now.'

The hint was taken, the subject dropped. 'You're not thinking of going back?'

'No way,' came the unequivocal reply. 'Only you tell me what I'm supposed to do with this . . .' jerking a thumb in Ria's direction, 'short of dropping him overboard!'

'I already told you I was more than willing to work

my passage,' put in Ria, eager to get things on a proper footing.

'You haven't told me anything yet,' he growled. 'But that's about to be rectified. We'll make a start with the name.'

'Is it important?' she stalled. 'It won't mean anything to you.'

'It might mean something to the authorities when I hand you over.'

Her heart gave a downward lurch. 'You wouldn't do that?'

'Depends on what you come up with. I'm not turning a kid like you loose in Brunei without good reason, that's for sure.'

'I'm joining my stepmother,' she said in swift inspiration. 'Is that good enough?'

'It might be if I believed it.'

'Why should you disbelieve it?'

There was a pause, another faint furrowing of dark brows as he raked a glance over her. 'Take off the cap,' he ordered suddenly.

Sooner or later, Ria reminded herself as she slowly obeyed. She saw the grey eyes narrow still further, heard Mike's soft exclamation.

'Now the jacket.' Ty Morgan curled a lip when she hesitated. 'Mike.'

'All right.' She held up a staying hand as the younger man started towards her. 'You don't have to prove anything. My name is Ria Brownlow.'

'How did you guess?' asked Mike in tones of bemusement. 'I thought he was pretty skinny for a boy, but it never occurred to me he might be female!'

'It takes a female to answer every damned question with another,' came the sardonic comment. 'Plus the voice kept rising an octave. Take over for me.'

Ria steadied her nerve as he indicated the hatch she had recently used. If he wanted her story he should have it. It might arouse some sympathy for her cause. She preceded him down the companionway, opening

the door to the saloon and passing through without
being told.

There was an aroma in the air that made her
suddenly conscious of the gnawing emptiness inside her.
'Do you think I could have some coffee?' she asked as
Captain Morgan followed her into the cabin. 'I haven't
eaten in almost twenty-four hours, apart from a few
biscuits.'

'Taken from here, I suppose,' he said, moving
towards the galley. 'Thought the tin seemed to be going
down fast. Sit down and get ready to talk. And I want
the truth.'

There was no point in fabrication, Ria conceded.
What she had to do was make the truth sound plausible
enough to be believed. It wasn't going to be all that
easy.

CHAPTER TWO

TY MORGAN looked at home in the galley, lighting one of the burners and setting a blue enamel pot to heat before taking down mugs from an overhead rack. The milk was dried, of course. He spooned in sugar without bothering to ask her preferences. Not that it mattered; Ria could take it or leave it.

'So shoot,' he invited. 'From the beginning.'

She took a deep breath before complying, trying to keep her tone level as she recounted the happenings of the past few weeks. He listened without comment, bringing across the coffee when it was good and hot, and taking a seat himself.

'You're crazy,' he stated flatly when she had brought him up to date. 'What was wrong with asking the proper authorities to look the woman up for you?'

'It would have cost too much to organise, for one thing,' she said. 'Apart fom which, it wasn't what my father wanted. Whichever way you look at it, Jemo and her son are family. I have to see them for myself.'

'Have you any idea what conditions in Sarawak are like? That's rainforest up there. The only way in is by river, and that isn't any picnic.'

'I don't expect it to be,' Ria defended stoutly. 'I read everything I could lay my hands on about the area—in addition to what my father told me about it.'

'A dying man doesn't see all that straight. It's no place for a girl on her own, you can take *my* word for that.'

'I can take care of myself.'

'Yeah?' The tone was frankly sceptical. 'What do you weigh—eight stone?'

'Eight and a half.'

'Oh, makes all the difference!'

Her jaw went rigid. 'Size isn't the be-all and end-all!'

'Where you're thinking of going, sex might be. How would you fancy fetching up as some *penghulu*'s delight?'

'That's a tribal chief, isn't it?' she queried, refusing to rise to the bait. 'They're not savages any more.'

'No? The Ibans were still taking heads as recently as '66.'

'Only because they misunderstood British military tactics,' on a scornful note. 'You won't scare me that way.'

The laugh was short. 'It won't matter anyway. You won't be allowed into the interior on your own.'

'Then I'll have to go without permission, won't I?'

He studied her a moment before replying, mouth twisted. 'I can't make my mind up whether you're as naïve as you're making out or just plain bloody-minded,' he said at length. 'The Rajang's a few hundred miles from Brunei, for starters, then it could take a week or more to make it up-river, depending on conditions. For another thing, the Ukit longhouses are over the Indonesian side.'

'Apart from a couple of small settlements,' Ria insisted. 'My father knew what he was talking about. He spent more than a year in Borneo.'

'Sure. And I've been sailing the South China seas for three. So what? The best thing you can do is fly back to Singapore from Brunei, then hightail it home. You might have to wait a couple of days, but it's reasonably civilised.' He drained the coffee-mug, added with deliberation, 'In the meantime, you'd better start earning your keep. Jack will be more than willing to turn over the cooking and bottle-washing for a few days. And take off that damned jacket before you melt. We don't run to air-conditioning.'

Ria fumbled with the buttons, fingers unaccustomedly clumsy under his gaze. She was wearing a thin cotton shirt beneath, the latter clinging to her damp skin. A gleam of derision appeared in the grey eyes as he studied the outline of her small, firm breasts.

'Not exactly what you'd call well endowed,' he commented, 'but not so boyish either. Did you cut your hair yourself?'

'I always wear my hair short,' she said. 'It's easier to manage.' She felt stifled, self-conscious to a degree she had never experienced before. 'Can't we forget the sex thing?'

'Treat you like one of the guys, you mean?' He shrugged easily. 'If that's what you want. You can share my cabin. Mike and Jack have the other.' The derision increased at her change of expression. 'You can't have it both ways. Right now, I'm fighting a powerful impulse to leather the hell out of you, so just watch your step!'

Ria said stiffly, 'I was telling the truth up there. I'm no kid!'

'Age has nothing to do with it. You need to do some growing up—and fast.'

She was getting nowhere like this, Ria told herself, biting back the hasty retort. Here was a man accustomed to having his own way in every sphere. If she wanted to better him she was going to have to employ the feminine tactics she had always despised. The first step was to stop arguing her case.

She waited a brief moment or two as if considering before making a sudden rueful little gesture. 'All right, you made your point. I should have stayed at home. I'm sorry for putting you on the spot like this. You've every right to be angry.'

Whether he was taken in or not was in no way certain. 'You'd better get yourself something to eat,' he said. 'We don't want you keeling over.'

'Thanks. If you'll tell me what you want, I'll make a start on lunch.'

'We only eat a full cooked meal once a day in the evening. The rest of the time we manage on snacks. You'll find plenty of tinned stuff in the bottom locker, perishables in the fridge. We're none of us choosy when it comes to food.'

'Perhaps as well,' she said, summoning a smile, 'because I'm no gourmet cook. You can leave me to it if you want to get back to the bridge, captain.'

'Make it Ty,' he suggested drily.

'Ty, then.' She rose with him, holding out her hand for the empty mug he was still holding. This close he towered over her, making her feel suddenly and oddly vulnerable. His skin had a healthy sheen to it, the muscle taut and hard below the surface. The brush of his fingers against hers sent a tremor the length of her arm: she drew back as if stung. 'About the sleeping arrangements ...' she got out, and saw his lips tilt again.

'Changed your mind about that too?'

'I can bed down right here,' she said. 'The seating is meant as extra berth space, isn't it?'

'Sure. Not much privacy, though.'

'I can manage.'

'Maybe. We'll work something out.'

He left her then, closing the bulkhead door behind him. Ria took both mugs through to the galley and stacked them on the side of the sink ready for washing later. As he had said, there was no shortage of food. All it needed was a little imagination. Mugs of thick vegetable soup followed by stacks of sandwiches would probably do for lunch; dinner was going to be more of a problem. With three or four days to get through, she was going to need every ounce of ingenuity she possessed—and not only where eating was concerned either. Somehow or other she had to get Ty Morgan on her side, even, if necessary, enlist his help. She hadn't come all this way in order to turn meekly round and go home again just because one man said she should. One way or another, she was going to find what she had set out to find.

She was half-way through a sandwich of her own when Mike put in an appearance via the aft companionway. He pursed his lips in a soundless little whistle when he saw her standing there in front of the port away from which she had just turned.

'Definitely female,' he remarked. 'Don't know how I missed it!'

'If you're looking for food,' Ria said severely, 'lunch won't be ready for another half-hour.'

'Food can wait. First time we ever had a girl on board. The skipper doesn't believe in mixing business with pleasure.'

'He still doesn't,' she responded. 'I'm here on sufferance.'

'And some. I've been warned to stay away from you.'

'It doesn't seem to have had much effect.'

His grin was designed to appeal. 'A deaf ear comes in useful now and then. That's some story you told him.'

'It happens to be the truth.'

He considered her for a moment, head on one side, eyes calculating. 'Guess it's just about crazy enough, at that. I only ever saw one Ukit woman, but she sure had what it takes to turn a man's head!'

Ria said quickly, 'Malaysian or Indonesian side of the border?'

'What? Oh, the woman, you mean? Malaysian. Never did find out what she was doing as far down-river as Sibu.'

Sudden excitement coursed through her veins. 'That's on the Rajang, isn't it?'

'That's right. We're doing the same run this trip. And if you're thinking you might persuade him to take you with us, forget it. He'll turn you in as soon as we make port, that's for sure. The authorities there won't mess about either. You'll be shipped out straight away as an undesirable.' The grin came again. 'Not that I'd agree with 'em on that score!'

Ria turned a deaf ear of her own to the last. She'd met his type before, and found them just as boring. She wasn't going to give up hope. Not yet awhile. If all else failed, she'd slip over the side before they reached harbour and make her own way to Sarawak, with or without papers.

'I'll just have to wait and see what happens,' she said, moving towards the galley. 'I take it there are just the three of you on board?'

'Four now. A nice round figure. Talking of round figures,' he added, 'did anybody ever tell you you've got a real neat little tail end yourself?'

'Not until now.' She didn't even bother to turn round. 'Don't you have anything to do?'

'Nothing that can't wait.' His tone altered a fraction, taking on a softer note. 'Be friendly and I might find a way to help you out.'

'You don't waste any time, do you?' she said scathingly over a shoulder. 'I'm not interested in your kind of friendship, thanks!'

'Not a dyke, are you?'

'No, I'm not!' She should have treated the question with the contempt it deserved, Ria acknowledged the moment the denial was out, but it was too late. Eyes frosty, she tagged on, 'If you don't get out of here I'll call Captain Morgan and tell him what you just said.'

He shrugged. 'Can't blame a man for trying. Just hope you can cook.'

Silly to get upset because of some yobbo who thought he was God's gift to women, Ria told herself as he left the same way he had come. With his rakish good looks, the mate very likely found most conquests easy. He did nothing for her at all, but that was nothing new. She had yet to meet a man who could make her feel in any way inclined towards a physical relationship. The few times she had been kissed had either been under protest or because she hadn't wanted to hurt someone's feelings too much.

There was a mirror fastened to the bulkhead over the sink. She studied her reflection for a moment, a faint line drawn between her brows. Free of any trace of make-up, the face that gazed back at her was too familiar to hold any surprises: blue eyes, a small straight nose, too-wide mouth and stubborn chin. She rarely thought about her looks at all; she certainly wasn't going to start worrying about her image now. One thing she was certain about, she was not attracted to other girls.

Mike, she was glad to find, was taking his stint at the helm when lunchtime arrived. Jack took food up to him, returning to attack his own portion with a gusto Ria would not have thought possible after the previous night's excesses. Neither he nor Ty made any comment about the food. There wasn't, she wryly acknowledged, a great deal one could say about soup and sandwiches. She had found a large chicken ready plucked and drawn in the kerosene-run refrigerator. That, together with some of the fresh vegetables, was going to form the basis of the evening meal.

With no hot water on tap, washing up took her some time. It was almost two o'clock by the time she put the last dish away and tidied the galley. The heat was tangible. She would have given a great deal for a cool shower. Toilet facilities on board were, to say the least, limited.

Venturing up on deck, she found Jack sitting on the hatch cover whittling away at a piece of wood. He was making a model of the *Tiger Rose*, he told her. This was to be the bridge housing when it was finished.

'I'm going to have a lot more time for it while you're on board,' he declared comfortably. 'The skipper said to leave you to it.'

Ria smiled and shrugged. 'I'm not complaining. I was always prepared to earn my passage.' She hesitated before adding, 'I suppose he's told you why I want to get to Borneo?'

'The bare bones of it.' He gave her a shrewd glance. 'He's right, you know. You'd never make it on your own.'

'You mean I'd need a man with me?'

'It'd help.'

'Do you know of anybody in Brunei who might take me up-river?'

'I know plenty who'd jump at the chance to have a girl like you all to themselves for a week or two,' was the blunt reply. 'You've been lucky so far. Don't go pushing it.'

'I can't go back,' Ria protested. 'Not without making some attempt.'

'You might not have any choice.'

She was silent, contemplating the turquoise seascape. The surface was almost flat calm, the sun beating down from a sky hazy with heat. Far off on the horizon a faint plume of smoke signalled the presence of some large vessel on a parallel course. Apart from that, they had the ocean to themselves.

'How long have you been with Captain Morgan?' she asked after a moment or two.

'Coming up four years. We met up in Madagascar. He was running an old tug then. Found this old girl in a breaker's yard in Bombay and spent six months restoring her. We've run cargoes as far up as Shanghai and down to Papua without any trouble.'

'Mike too?'

'No, he's only been around a few months. The last mate got himself tied up with a woman in Manila. She soon put paid to his sailing days!'

Ria said softly, 'As senior member of the crew, shouldn't you have been offered the position?'

'Never got my ticket. Wouldn't have wanted it, anyway. I keep things shipshape. You won't find a cleaner boat than the *Tiger* in these parts, I can tell you!'

'I noticed that last night.'

There was a slight pause. Jack looked suddenly uncomfortable. 'About last night,' he said. 'It was you who got me on board, wasn't it?'

She kept her eyes to the front. 'Yes.'

He sighed. 'Thought I'd dreamt it till I saw you up on the bridge this morning. Thanks for not letting on. I was supposed to be on watch. Just slipped ashore for a couple of bottles, only one thing led to another . . .' He stopped and shrugged, expression wry.

'You don't have any family yourself?'

'A couple of cousins back in Manchester, maybe. I've been bumming round the world since I was in my twenties. Never found anywhere I wanted to settle. I owe a whole lot to the skipper. I was a regular down and out when he found me in Tamatave.'

'Saviour of souls!' she murmured caustically.

'Don't knock him,' he defended. 'You could have landed in a whole heap of trouble taking the kind of chance you took. There's some who'd have had you paying for your passage every which way, believe me!'

The mate being one of them, no doubt, she reflected. Lucky for her the captain didn't fancy his chances too. The sudden *frisson* along her spine was accompanied by an involuntary tensing of stomach muscles. Goose walking over her grave, she told herself. She hoped it wasn't an omen.

Supper turned out to be an unqualified success, the pot-roasted chicken so tender it fell off the bone. Gratified by its reception Ria followed it up with a fruit crumble and custard. Now that they were clear of the main shipping lines the wheel could be lashed, enabling the whole crew at least to eat together. A three-way watch would still apparently be kept at night.

'She could put you out of a job if you're not careful, Jack,' observed Mike at the end of the meal. 'More decorative, too!'

'And who'd play nursemaid to that bloody engine through there?' demanded the older man, bristling at the taunt. 'You might have the qualifications, but I'm the only one she'll run sweet for!'

'Don't let's start a free-for-all.' Ty sounded easy enough but the authority was there all the same. 'And watch the language. We've a lady on board.'

'Don't mind me,' said Ria levelly. 'I've heard worse. Does everybody want coffee?'

'You can bring me mine up top.' Ty was already getting to his feet. 'Just make sure the valves are turned right off when you've finished using the burners. We don't want kerosene leaking all over the deck.'

'I've used pressurised stoves before,' she responded, trying to keep the sarcasm from showing in her voice. 'Don't worry about it.'

Humour touched the firm mouth for a fleeting moment. 'A real little all-rounder! I suppose we could have done worse.'

Mike laughed. 'We sure could!'

Ria ignored both comments, busying herself with the coffee. Jack was the only one of the three she could talk to in any real sense—the only one of the three who might be persuaded to help her out, if it came to that. Mike would no doubt have been ready enough with his promises had she been willing to play along with him, but just as ready to dump her once he had had what he wanted if she was any judge of character at all. Ty was the real enigma. He didn't fit any accepted pattern. The little Jack had told her about him had only served to whet her curiosity for more.

He was studying charts and smoking a cheroot when she took the coffee up to the bridge.

'Thanks,' he said absently, indicating a space. 'Just stick it down there.'

Putting down the mug, Ria found herself reluctant to leave, moving instead to look out through the screen at the long slow swell. The sky was clear overhead, the moon almost full. Phosphorescence sparkled in the bow waves.

'It's so peaceful,' she murmured. 'I didn't expect it to be as calm as this.'

'It isn't always,' Ty responded without turning round. 'There's a force seven on its way, so don't get complacent.'

'Fat chance of that with you around.' Her tone was disgruntled. 'I realise you think I'm next door to an idiot, but . . .'

'I don't think you're an idiot,' he interrupted.

'Foolhardy, maybe, but you've got your wits about you.'

'I suppose I should be grateful for that much of a concession!'

He laid down the pencil and slide rule, leaning an elbow against the table top as he cradled the coffee-mug. 'I've made more than one concession where you're concerned. Whether I keep on making them is up to you.'

She let the pause stand for a moment before saying softly, 'Mike tells me you're going up the Rajang this trip.'

'Mike talks too much.' His tone had hardened. 'It wouldn't do you any good, anyway. We only go as far as Sibu. It takes a couple of days just to get up to Belaga from there. The place you're looking for is another two or three days' up the Barang Balui on top of that.'

Her eyes widened a fraction. 'You know Long Laha?'

'Only by name. I took a trip up to Long Busang one time. That's the next village along—the last one before the border. Travel is by longboat.'

'Dad said when he was there they still had a couple of the old *River Queens* in service. They're not all that primitive.'

'They mightn't have been when they were built, they're about on their last legs now.' He shook his head impatiently. 'You can't even be sure the woman's still there.'

'If she isn't they'll know where she's gone.' Ria seized on the opening, slight though it was. 'Dad told me the *orang ulu* were mostly to be trusted. That means country people, doesn't it? I suppose they haven't had as much chance to learn the white man's evil ways as the coastal tribes.'

The smile was reluctant. 'You could be right about that. It's still no place for a woman.'

She said slyly, 'I'm gaining *some* ground at least!'

'A slip of the tongue,' he denied. 'Don't let it go to

your head.' He paused, eyeing her consideringly, then seemed to come to some decision. 'Look, supposing I took you down the coast as far as Miri and you gave the authorities there the details? If she's still in Sarawak they'll find her a hell of a sight quicker than you could.'

'And then what?' she asked. 'How much of the money Dad left for her would be likely to reach her if I simply handed it over?'

'It's a chance you'd have to take.'

'It's one I'm not prepared to take.'

He said roughly. 'You just don't know when to give up, do you?'

'If there's no challenge, it isn't worth doing.' Ria waited a moment, watching him, registering the uncompromising line of mouth and jaw. 'I made a promise,' she appealed. 'I can't go back on it without exploring every avenue. If you think it would be dangerous for me to travel alone, then help me find somebody trustworthy to take me.'

He picked up the smouldering cheroot and drew on it before answering, his gaze penetrating. Ria couldn't bring herself to look away. She felt knotted up inside, conscious of heat spreading through her body, of a strange weakness in her limbs. Her heart was thudding, her throat as dry as a bone. She swallowed hard, wondering if she was sickening for something. It would be just her luck!

'I'll say one thing for you,' Ty stated on an odd note, 'you're not short on guts.'

She said thickly, 'Does that mean you'll let me come with you up-river?'

'It means I'll think about it.' He turned abruptly back to the chart table. 'You'll be using my cabin. I'll take the saloon. Now get out of here.'

Ria forced herself to move. It was more than she had anticipated—more than she probably deserved. Not that it was in the bag yet, by any means. He could still decide to dump her in Brunei.

CHAPTER THREE

LIFE settled into a routine of sorts over the following two days. Ria was awake at six and in her berth again before ten. Between times, she found plenty to occupy both mind and hands.

There had been no further opportunity to discuss her immediate future with Ty. If anything, he seemed to go out of his way to avoid being alone with her. Mike made no such effort, although he appeared to have accepted her lack of interest in his initial offer. He could be extremely entertaining when he set out to be, she found. He had done five years in the Merchant Navy before deciding to go freelance: the *Tiger Rose* was only the latest in a whole line of berths since. He had no particular ambition to better his status by acquiring a craft of his own. Ownership carried too many risks.

The weather was back to hot and calm again after twenty-four hours of rough seas. Ria had been relieved to find her sea-legs holding up. Cooking was the only job allocated to her. Apart from that she was free to please herself. There were plenty of books on board, most of them in the cabin she was using. A great many of these concerned the sea in one guise or another, but there were enough anomalies to create more questions in her mind regarding Ty's background. What kind of man read pure mathematics for leisure-time entertainment?

Flying fish abounded in these latitudes, silvery shafts of light clearing the surface in leaps which lasted as much as ten seconds. There were porpoise too. Sometimes a whole school of them would accompany the ship for miles. Ria loved to stand at the bow-rail watching the creatures keeping pace. They themselves seemed to thoroughly enjoy the pastime, often arching right out of the water in a display of sheer exuberance. When it came to speed, they could beat the *Tiger Rose* hands down.

'I envy you this life,' Ria said to Jack on the third afternoon when he came to join her at the rail for a moment or two. 'If I were a man, I could think of nothing better.'

'There are some women sailors,' he said idly. 'The Russians even let them skipper a ship if they're good enough.'

Ria laughed. 'Not quite what I had in mind.' There was a pause. When she spoke again it was on a more sober note. 'I'm beginning to realise what I took on making this trip. It all seemed just a big adventure back at home.'

Jack gave her a sidelong glance. 'Having second thoughts?'

'About completing it?' She shook her head. 'I'll see it through, one way or another.' This time the pause was briefer. 'Did Ty say anything to you about taking me all the way?'

'No, but that's not to say he won't.'

'You think there's a chance?'

'There's always a chance.' It was Jack's turn to shake his head. 'I've known the skipper a long time, but don't ask me to read his mind. If you want to know what he's decided to do, you'll have to ask him yourself.'

'I would,' she said wryly, 'if I could get to see him alone for five minutes.'

'He's on the bridge. Why not try him now?'

'Because he made it clear yesterday that I was in the way.'

'Considering the weather, I'm not surprised. The last thing he needed right then was a distraction.'

'I'm hardly that.'

Lined features creased in a grin. 'Don't count on it. You might be only a bit of a thing, but what you've got is in all the right places. Can't understand how either of 'em got mistook in the first place!'

'You did,' Ria pointed out.

'I wasn't seeing too well at the time.' He was studying her as he spoke. 'You'd be a real looker if you let your hair grow a bit and got into some female gear. Have all the fellers after you!'

Her chin lifted. 'I'm not interested in attracting men!'

'Garn!' The tone was derisive. 'You're not fooling me. I've seen the way you watch Ty when you think he's not looking. Big man, isn't he? Women go for his type.'

Ria made herself relax, accepting the fact that she was being teased. 'I didn't imagine he went short of female company.'

'Not so as you'd notice.' His tone altered. 'Mike neither, only he doesn't know where to draw the line.'

She glanced at the little man swiftly. 'Are you trying to tell me something?'

'Just not to encourage him too much.'

Her colour rose a fraction. 'I already made it clear there's nothing doing.'

'You talk with him, though. He might think you're just playing hard to get.'

'Are you sure,' she asked softly, 'you're not letting your dislike of him colour your judgment?'

He shrugged. 'Maybe. I never did cotton to him.'

'Ty obviously did.'

'Ty took him on for his seamanship. He knows his stuff, I'll grant you that.' Jack straightened away from the rail where he had been leaning at her side. 'Anyway, just think about it.'

'I will,' she promised, and smiled. 'Thanks for the concern, Jack. I appreciate it.'

'Somebody's got to look out for you,' he growled.

Ria stayed where she was as he moved on. If she went to make some coffee as an excuse for going up on to the bridge, she was probably going to run into Mike. After what Jack had just said, she wondered if it really had been wise to let down her guard where the mate was concerned. Leopards didn't change their spots. Not that he was likely to make any serious advances, of course.

She would only have to yell to have help at hand. All the same, it wouldn't hurt to be a little more careful in her dealings with him. They were due to reach port in Brunei early tomorrow morning, but if Ty did consent to let her stay on board right through to Sibu it was going to mean another two days at least.

If. That was the operative word. She could wait until he chose to tell her his decision, or she could forestall him by asking. Jack was right, she had chosen the wrong time yesterday. Ty had had enough on his hands just steering the ship through the wind-driven seas. He had ordered her brusquely below. Since then he had scarcely spoken to her at all. She had to make some attempt to get through to him while there was still a chance.

She could catch a glimpse of the dark head on the other side of the windscreen when she looked up. Taking her courage in both hands, she moved aft to mount the iron companionway. The door at the top was already open to allow free passage of air into the oven that was the interior of the bridge. Ty was stripped to the waist, his lower half clad only in a pair of faded khaki shorts. The explosion of hair on his chest thinned considerably where it met his waistband, revealing ridged muscle.

'All right if I come in?' Ria asked tentatively.

He didn't even glance in her direction. 'No reason why not.'

Stepping over the threshold, she moved to stand at his side, conscious of the lean brown strength in the hands holding the wheel.

'I'm sorry about yesterday,' she ventured after a moment. 'It was stupid of me to bother you at a time like that.'

He made no attempt to offer comfort in the way of polite denials. Not that she would have expected it, anyway. 'Is that it?' he asked.

'You know it isn't!' She bit her lip, modifying her tone. 'If it's going to be no, I wish you'd tell me.'

'So you can make plans to jump ship the first chance you get?' He gave her an oblique glance when she failed to reply. 'You've thought about it, haven't you?'

'It had crossed my mind,' she admitted. 'I'm a good swimmer.'

'You'd need to be more than that to outswim a hungry shark.'

'It's a risk I'd be prepared to take—unless you're planning on clapping me in irons.'

'That crossed *my* mind.'

She searched the strong features, heart leaping in sudden hope. 'Are you going to let me come with you?'

'Against my better judgment,' he conceded. 'And on one condition.'

'Anything,' she promised, and drew a sardonic lift of a brow.

'Try caution for a change. You don't know what I'm going to be asking for.'

Her heart thudded again, painfully this time. 'Anything within reason,' she amended on a suddenly husky note.

'That's better. I want your word that you'll hang around until we find somebody trustworthy to take you up-river. The local missionary might be a good place to start.'

The 'we' warmed her. 'You have it,' she said. 'And thanks.'

'I won't say my pleasure,' came the dry response, 'because it isn't. You're a lot of trouble whichever way I play it.'

'I know.' She could afford to laugh now that the danger was past. She felt buoyed up, full of confidence. 'I'm going to make you the finest chilli you ever tasted for supper tonight in celebration! It doesn't matter if I throw in every tin of mince I can find, does it?'

'No, we'll be stocking up again in Brunei.' Ty was smiling, albeit reluctantly. 'You're a better cook than I'd have given you credit for a while back.'

'I learned how to make a meal out of just about

anything on an Outward Bound course,' she said. 'I
don't know if you ever heard of those, but . . .'

'Sure I've heard of them. The D. of E. was awarding
gold medals long before I left England.'

'How long is it since you were in England?' Ria asked
curiously.

He shrugged. 'Five or six years—can't remember
exactly.'

'You've no family there?'

'Some.'

The slight hardening of tone warned her not to
pursue the subject any further. She said quickly, 'Is
steering a motorised ship very much different from
sail?'

'Why not try it?' he invited. 'It's calm enough.' He
relinquished his grasp of the wheel spokes even as he
said it, stepping back to allow her access. 'Bring her
back on sou' sou' east.'

The spokes felt warm beneath Ria's fingers, the
polished wood as smooth as silk. She concentrated on
the compass before her, very much aware of Ty's
closeness at her back, of the heat from his body as he
watched over her shoulder while she struggled to keep
the *Tiger Rose* on course.

'You're over-compensating,' he said after a few
minutes. 'The rudder doesn't answer as fast as on a
small sailboat, so allow for the lag.' His hands came
round to cover hers where they grasped the spokes,
correcting the drift. 'Like this.'

Ria tried her best to concentrate on what he was
saying, but her mind refused to grasp the import.
Encircled within his arms like this, she felt breathless,
excited, her insides churning. She had a sudden urgent
desire to lean back into the hardness of his chest, to feel
his arms wrapping her closer against him, the slight
roughness of his jaw rubbing her cheek. Her breasts
tingled, the nipples pushing against the thin material of
her shirt. There was a trembling weakness in her
thighs.

He had to know, she thought dazedly. This close, he had to be aware of what was happening to her. Almost as if in direct answer to the thought, he released her abruptly.

'I'll take her again,' he said. 'You must have other things to do.'

Ria muttered something and made her escape, leaning against the superstructure to regain her breath. Nothing she had ever experienced before had prepared her for the aching need penetrating to every part of her body. So this was what it felt like. No wonder it caused so much trouble. For a moment back there she would willingly have done anything he had wanted just to keep him with her. Only he hadn't wanted anything. To him she was just a kid he had promised to help. If he was not to withdraw that offer there must be no repeat of this afternoon's little episode. From now on she had to keep well away from him. Better for her, too, if it came to that.

She spent the rest of the afternoon washing through the few items of clothing she had brought along as spares. Despite the heat, she had not so far worn the single pair of shorts in her scanty wardrobe. She put them on now only because her jeans were badly in need of a scrub.

Everyone on board the *Tiger Rose* did their own laundry while at sea, hanging the articles out to dry on the after deck where a line was strung between two ventilating shafts. At present it was empty. Ria quickly pegged out her briefs and spare shirt, then hung up the dripping jeans. They would be dry by nightfall; she could change back again before supper. The idea of facing Ty in anything less was not to be countenanced. Not after this afternoon. He might even think she was attempting to entice him.

The feelings he had aroused in her were still there inside her, making her restless, on edge. It was like having an itch one couldn't scratch. She would get over it; she had to get over it. Even if Ty himself was willing to initiate her into the mysteries of sexual intercourse, it wasn't what she was here for. If nothing else, there was the morality angle to consider.

It wouldn't matter, came the thought, creeping into her mind despite all her efforts to keep it out. Where Ty Morgan was concerned, nothing mattered. She had never felt like this in her life before—perhaps she might never feel like it again.

'Need any help?' asked a voice behind her, making her jump. 'I'm ready, willing and able!'

Mike was standing a few feet away when she turned, his head to one side as he looked her over. 'Long-legged and lovely,' he remarked. 'That's some outfit!'

'It's all I've got left that's clean,' she said defensively.

'So who's complaining?' He lifted his eyes to hers, jaw suddenly clenching. 'Ria, I want you,' he said thickly. 'You're driving me crazy!'

She stiffened. 'I'm sorry. It isn't intentional.'

His laugh was harsh. 'Don't give me that. You know exactly what you do to a man with that wide-eyed innocent look of yours! You've been playing me along the whole way.'

'That's not true. I was simply trying to be sociable.' Ria set herself as he made a movement towards her ready to repel any effort on his part to take hold of her. 'If you touch me you'll regret it,' she warned.

Unexpectedly he smiled, holding up his hands in mock defence. 'O.K., if that's the way you want it!'

'That's exactly the way I want it.' She turned abruptly and walked away, thankful when he made no attempt to follow her. She had no doubts regarding her ability to stop any man who did make a grab at her, but it was always better to avoid conflict if at all possible. Jack had known what he was talking about. Fortunately the other man had been prepared to take no for an answer—this time. From now on she would be more careful in what she said and did.

The chilli went down well with all three men. Ria herself ate little of it.

'Not sickening for something, I hope?' queried Ty when she pushed away her plate.

'No,' she said, 'just not hungry.'

'I'll finish it for you,' offered Jack, reaching for the plate and adding the contents to his own with cheerful alacrity. 'Waste not want not, that's my motto!'

Ria got to her feet to take the empty plate through to the galley, catching Mike's eye as she did so and feeling her teeth clench as he winked. She hoped neither of the others had noticed. The confrontation was going to have to come eventually, there was nothing surer. Mike Lander was not a man to accept defeat on the strength of one rebuttal. The thing that worried her most was Ty's probable reaction to any trouble in that direction. It wouldn't take much to make him change his mind about taking her along.

She retired to her cabin at nine, pleading tiredness. Ty made no comment but his glance was weighted. He was aware something was bothering her, that was certain. If he asked she was going to have to make up some excuse. Pre-menstrual tension should cover it. She had never actually suffered from that particular malady herself, but she had heard it talked about often enough. The fact that she wasn't due for another two weeks was neither here nor there.

Rocked by the gentle swell, she read for a couple of hours before finally settling down to sleep. After only three days she felt totally at home on the *Tiger Rose*. It was going to be a real wrench to say goodbye to the ship—in more ways than one. Lying there, she let her thoughts drift, wondering how long it was going to take to find someone willing and able to accompany her into the Sarawak interior—and how much she might have to pay her guide when found. The slender wad of cash was back in the pocket of her jeans again after spending the afternoon hidden beneath her pillow. It might be an idea to change the large denomination notes for ones of smaller value when they reached Sibu, or Jemo might easily find herself cheated by the traders who plied their wares up-river from Belaga. Ty would be the one to ask for advice on that score. He knew the set-up.

Ty. No matter how she tried to avoid it, her thoughts always came back to him in the end. She could visualise him now in her mind's eye, broad shoulders tapering to narrow waist and hip, long, powerful legs, the sun-gilded lustre of his skin. Her body stirred restlessly. If only she were older, experienced, able to meet him on his own level. She had never blushed in her life before, yet she seemed to be doing it all the time when she was with Ty. He knew how he made her feel all right. A lesser man might easily have taken advantage of it, but not him. She only wished he would.

She came awake with a jerk some indefinable time later when the cabin door was softly opened. It took her a moment or two to gather her senses, by which time Mike had closed the door again and was half-way across the cabin.

'Get out of here!' Ria snapped, coming up on an elbow. 'I already told you . . .'

'You'll change your mind,' he said in low but confident tones. 'Just give me five minutes.'

'I wouldn't give you five seconds,' she grated, clutching the coarse white cotton sheet closer to her. 'Didn't I make myself clear enough this afternoon?'

'As day.' His eyes were gleaming in the moonlight filtering through the porthole. 'Only the game's gone on long enough. Better lie back and enjoy it, honey, because I'm not leaving without.'

The upper berth was lifted to the bulkhead, robbing her of even that much protection. Ria smiled suddenly and held out an inviting hand. 'I suppose you're right. It's time we got this sorted out.'

Mike grinned and made to take the hand, letting out a yell as her stiffened thumb jabbed deep into the radial nerve. Cursing, he clutched the numbed forearm, trying to work his paralysed fingers. Ria took advantage of the moment to slide from the bed and start for the door, still holding the sheet about her. Handicapped as she was, there was no point in waiting until he recovered from the shock. Pain such as she had just inflicted was scarcely scheduled to improve his outlook.

Ty was right outside when she flung the door open. He looked from her face to the man beyond her, jaw rigid.

'Come on out of it,' he ordered harshly.

Mike obeyed with obvious reluctance, shooting Ria a look of pure venom. His male pride would have suffered most, she reflected, trying to control her own trembling reaction to the incident. Perhaps after this he might take notice.

'Treading on your toes, am I?' he growled. 'Well, you're welcome!'

Ria stared after him as he went off towards the saloon, looking back at Ty with a growing hurt in her eyes. 'Is that all you're going to do?'

'You'd have liked to see me knock him down?' His tone was sardonic. 'A fight to the death maybe!'

She said fiercely, 'He tried to rape me!'

'Are you sure you don't mean make you? There's a difference.'

'I know what I mean.' The hurt had been replaced by anger, hot and furious. 'I should have expected you'd stick up for him. I suppose it was all my own fault?'

'Some of it, yes. You've been giving him enough rope.'

'That's unfair, and you know it!'

The grey eyes had a spark of their own. 'If you really believe that, it's about time somebody shook you up!'

Ria tried to turn her face away as he reached for her, but he grasped her chin and held it firm. The hard, demanding pressure of his lips was a physical shock. Involuntarily, she parted her own, feeling the swift run of fire through her veins.

The sheet was slipping, but she suddenly didn't care. There was no room for anything in her mind but the fact that Ty was holding her at last, kissing her with a force slowly changing character, his hands moving the length of her back to draw her up closer against him in a caress that made the blood thunder in her ears. She wanted to get closer, to melt into that rock-hard body, to feel his hands on her bare skin.

She kept her eyes closed when he lifted his head at last, too overwhelmed by the sensations running riot inside her to meet his eyes.

'Seems I was wrong,' he said roughly. 'You know what you're after, all right!'

The strength went out of her limbs as he slid an arm beneath her knees and lifted her. He was going to do the very same thing Mike had intended doing, only this time there was no reluctance, no distaste, because she wanted it too. More than anything else in the world!

It took him bare moments to carry her across to the berth. Laying her down, he went back to close and bolt the door. Dizzily, Ria watched him strip off his shirt and trousers, dropping them where he stood. She had never seen a man wholly naked before; she somehow hadn't anticipated doing so now. The sight of him sent waves of excitement through her body, starting at the very pit of her stomach and spreading outwards with every ragged breath. Even then there was no thought of drawing back. She loved this man, she thought mistily. It had to be love if he could make her feel like this. Making love was a right and proper extension of that emotion. She needed to know him all the way through.

She was wearing nothing beneath the wound sheet for the simple reason that it had been too hot to don the cotton pyjamas she had brought with her. There was a brief moment of resistance when Ty drew the covering material away from her, but it vanished in the electric thrill as his hand began a light, questing exploration of her slender curves, the leathery hardness of his palm in no way detracting from the sensitivity of his fingertips. When his lips followed the same path she could no longer contain the shuddering response, sliding her fingers into the dark hair to draw him closer, arching her back instinctively to lift her small, uptilted breasts to his mouth, a choked little cry wrung from her lips at the exquisite agony of his caress. She wanted it to stop, yet she still continued to hold him close, writhing and gasping beneath him, mind filled with nothing but this moment, this sensation, the urgency mounting within.

When he finally came over her she was eager in her reception, limbs pliant and supple in his grasp. A small part of her anticipated pain, but nothing like the splitting, tearing invasion of those first moments. Her whole body went rigid, fighting it, trying to escape. From somewhere far off she heard his roughened exclamation, felt his sudden stillness and then the deep groan as he started to move again. The pain faded, became part of the heat flaring out from that one central spark, growing and growing until it encapsulated every inch of her body, and she was moving with him, casting out restriction in the surging need for release, faster and faster until the fire exploded inside her and the whole world seemed to dissolve.

She came back to the reality of the narrow berth with reluctance, easing her cramped limbs beneath Ty's weight. Pushing himself abruptly upright, he ran a rough hand through his hair.

'Why didn't you stop me before it was too late?' he demanded gruffly. 'If I'd realised it was the first time ...' He broke off, jaw clenching. 'You came on so strong I was sure you had to know what it was all about!'

Ria said huskily, 'You mean you wouldn't have done it if you'd known I was still a virgin? I always understood that was what men liked.'

'Liked?' His lips twisted. 'Oh, sure, I liked it all right! Only there's a time and a place for everything, and this isn't it.'

Her throat hurt. 'Why not? It had to happen some time.'

'So why choose me for the privilege?' he asked on a

harsh note. 'If the experience was all you were after, why not Mike?'

'Because it wasn't like that.' She reached out timidly and touched his arm, feeling the muscle contract beneath her fingers. 'It really wasn't, Ty! I wanted you, not just anybody.'

'You thought I might be more gentle about it?'

'It wasn't your fault you hurt me,' she said. 'Anyway, it didn't last long.' She added defiantly, 'And it was worth it.'

'Sure,' he said again.

'I mean it.' She paused a moment, searching for the right words. 'Ty, I never felt like this about anybody before. You've got to believe that. I think I'm in love with you.'

The curse was muttered but no less meaningful. 'Don't talk rot!' he said forcefully. 'You don't know anything about me.'

'I know enough. I don't care about the rest.'

He shook his head, the faint smile reluctant. 'Anybody ever tell you you're not supposed to lay it all out on the line like that?'

Ria smiled back, relieved by the slackening of tension, slight though it was. 'I never could understand why people have to be so secretive about their feelings. I don't expect you to love me back—oh, it would be wonderful if you did, of course, but it isn't essential.'

He was looking at her as if he'd never seen her before, expression bemused. 'That's an unusual philosophy for a woman.'

A woman. Yes, she reflected with a little thrill of emotion, she really could call herself that now! Her body stirred afresh at the memory. The second time was always better—where had she read that?

Ty dropped his gaze from her face to her breasts, mouth contracting afresh. 'Cover yourself up,' he ordered with sudden brusqueness, and reached for his own clothing. 'The sooner I get out of here the better.'

'Why?' she whispered. 'What difference can it make now?'

'Enough.' He stood up to pull the denim trousers over lean hips, sliding the zip with a forceful sound. 'One mistake is enough.'

'You mean you don't want me any more?'

His laugh was low and lacking in humour. 'I want you.'

'Then stay with me.'

He stopped what he was doing for a moment to look at her, eyes almost angry. 'The last thing I needed was this! You're too young for me Ria. You don't belong out here.'

'I'm no younger than I was a few minutes ago.'

'We're not talking about the same thing. You need looking after.'

Alarm flared through her. 'You're still going to take me to Sibu?'

'I don't know.'

She came up on her knees, heedless of her nudity. 'You said you would! You can't go back on it now!'

'I can do anything I damned well think fit,' he came back tautly. 'And for God's sake, will you get something on!'

She snatched up the sheet, anger mingling with hurt. 'It's all true, isn't it?' she flashed. 'I'm nothing now you've had what you wanted! Well, go ahead. Turn me in to the authorities when we get to Brunei. Only I wonder how they're going to react when I tell them how I was raped by the brave captain of the *Tiger Rose!*'

His smile was grim. 'You'd have a job proving it, even if they were prepared to take notice. The general opinion would most likely be that you asked for it. Stowaways have to accept the risks.'

The anger went out of her suddenly, leaving her bitterly ashamed of her outburst. 'I'm sorry,' she said. 'I didn't really mean it, Ty. I wanted you to make love to me.'

He was silent, watching her, conflicting expressions crossing tense features. The sigh came from deep down. 'Ria, don't get me wrong. Believe me, it isn't that I don't feel anything. You crawled right up under my skin that first morning. You've more spirit than any other girl I ever came across, but you're still unbelievably young in a lot of ways—and a romantic. If I take you with us this is more than likely going to happen again. I can't afford to get involved. I don't *want* to get involved. Try and understand what I'm saying.'

'I do.' She felt wretched, her chest aching. 'I really do understand, Ty. Only please reconsider. I won't bother you again, I promise. I'll stay right away from you.'

'It isn't that big a ship,' he returned drily.

'So I'll stay right here in the cabin until we dock. Anything you say, if you'll only let me come.' She was desperate, aware that she herself had been the one to ruin everything. 'You said yourself I'd never get permission to travel on my own.'

'Which means you're going to be no worse off than you would have been if you'd got to Brunei by a normal route.' He shook his head. 'I'm sorry, but that's the way it is.'

Ria drew in a deep steadying breath. 'You owe me that much. You could have walked away from me.'

His own breath came out hard. 'It was a bit too late for that by the time I realised what I should have walked away from!'

'It makes no difference,' she insisted. 'If you're half the man I think you are, you'll keep your word.'

Grey eyes narrowed threateningly. 'You're in no fit state to be risking a hiding!'

Her chin jutted. 'You can't relegate me to the ranks again that way, either. You're not the only one round here with a ready knee!'

His mouth twitched suddenly, his expression relaxing for a moment into genuine if reluctant humour. 'There's just no putting you down, is there?'

There was one way, came the thought, instantly relegated to the very back of her mind where it could do the least trouble. There would be time enough later to lick her wounds. Right now she had other matters to concern her. She risked one more appeal. 'Please, Ty. I've come too far to just turn round and go home.'

He finished fastening his shirt buttons before answering, face enigmatic again, 'If I say yes, it has to be on the same condition as before. You wait for a proper guide.'

'Of course. Anything you say.'

'You can stop saying that for starters,' he retorted grimly. 'We're going to forget tonight ever happened. Right?'

The pain inside her contradicted that statement, but she said it anyway. 'Right.'

'Good.' He made a movement towards the door. 'I'm going back up top. I should have stayed there the first time.'

'Why did you come down?' Ria asked softly as he drew the bolt, and he turned back to look at her, a crooked little smile on his lips.

'I sensed trouble. I didn't realise it was going to be mine.'

Hers too, she thought as the door closed behind him. Both body and mind felt bruised. In a few hours they would be landing in Brunei. It was nobody's fault but her own that the prospect no longer inspired her.

CHAPTER FOUR

LAND appeared first as a green ribbon breaking the endless blue of sea and sky. Ria went up on deck when the *Tiger Rose* entered the wide estuary leading to Brunei's harbour, standing at the starboard rail to catch distant glimpses of mangrove swamp and dense forest, of the occasional cluster of stilted houses along the mudflats.

It was almost exactly as her imagination had painted it, the air vibrating with insect life, the heat palpable, the colours so sharp and clear they hurt the eye. Five years was a long time by the standards of the outside world, but here no more than a moment. She doubted if anything much would have altered since her father had been here himself.

Immigration officials came aboard when they docked, revealing no more than a passing interest in Ria's presence. The *Tiger Rose* was obviously a frequent enough visitor to these shores to deem any bureaucratic probing unnecessary. In all probability, she told herself drily, they took it for granted that she was the captain's woman. She had seen little enough of Ty since he had left her cabin last night. Jack had taken him breakfast up on the bridge. He wasn't exactly avoiding her, she knew. There was simply too much to do. Act as if nothing had happened, he had said. It was going to be difficult when her whole body ached for him the way it did.

Mike was surly this morning, prepared neither to forgive nor forget, it seemed. Whether he was aware that Ty had taken up where he had left off, Ria neither knew nor cared. He would get over last night a whole lot quicker than she would herself.

It was left to Jack to rouse her from her apathy,

coming down to the galley where she was wondering
what to prepare for a late lunch.

'We're taking a trip into town,' he announced. 'Want
to come?'

'Who's we?' she asked cautiously.

'Me and Ty.'

'Does he know you're asking me along?'

'Well, sure he does.' Jack gave her a suddenly
narrowed glance. 'It was his suggestion.'

Her mood lightened a little. Any concession was
better than nothing. 'In that case, yes, I would.'

'You'd be cooler in those shorts you were wearing
yesterday,' he advised. 'It's going to be scorching
ashore.'

He was wearing shorts himself. So, Ria surmised, was
Ty. She nodded. 'I'll go and change and meet you on
deck. Five minutes?'

'Fine, providing it is.'

She made it in four, to find both men waiting at the
head of the short gangway. Of Mike there was no sign.
Ty gave her a cursory glance which revealed nothing of his
thoughts, and led the way on to the wharf. Following
him, Ria took herself strictly in hand. There were going
to be no long silences on her part during this
expedition, no sidelong glances begging for his
attention. If he wanted to act as if last night had never
happened then she had to do the same.

They took a small outboard motorboat across the
bay with its floating petrol station, heading in under a
low, narrow-spanned bridge. The thoroughfare was as
busy as any city street, though with little perceptible
traffic system. Fast motor launches skirted slower
moving craft laden with fruit and vegetables, casting
mountains of spray in their passage. No one seemed to
care much about getting wet. In this climate clothing
dried again in minutes.

The town itself was surprisingly modern—rebuilt
after being badly bombed during World War Two, Jack
advised when Ria commented on the fact. The

magnificent mosque of Omar Saifuddin was the largest in the whole of South-east Asia, the museum holding the same record. There were apartment buildings, hotels, a huge shopping centre and even a sports stadium.

Alongside lay the older section called Kampong Ayer, where thousands of Malays still lived in small houses built on stilts along the inlets of the river. The government had been trying for years to persuade these people to move on to the mainland, said Jack, who appeared to have taken it on himself to act the part of guide and mentor on Ria's behalf, but they were still meeting with resistance. Tradition died hard here. In Sarawak she was going to find conditions much more primitive.

Ria listened with only half an ear. Ty had left them the moment they had landed, saying he had to see someone. It could be business, of course, but somehow she doubted it. A woman in every port, wasn't that the sailor's way? Malaysian, perhaps, or even Chinese. The thought of what he might be doing right now was tearing her apart.

They had stopped to eat at one of the waterside restaurants before meeting up with Ty again to return to the ship. The food was delicious, but Ria could do no more than toy with it.

'You *are* sickening for something,' stated Jack on a concerned note, watching her pick listlessly among the dozen or more small dishes. 'You had all the jabs before you set off on this jaunt of yours, I hope?'

'Of course I did.' She made an effort to smile and shrug. 'It must be the heat.'

'Yeah?' He sounded suddenly sceptical. 'Or maybe you're just feeling down because the company isn't what you'd like.'

Blue eyes lifted, anxious to dispel any unintentional hurt. 'It's nothing like that, Jack. You're wonderful company! I've really enjoyed today.'

'Don't go overboard,' he responded drily. 'All I'm

saying is you've been off the hooks ever since Ty took off. Expecting him to come along with us, weren't you?'

'I wasn't expecting anything,' she denied without expression. 'Not from him.'

'Like that, is it?' He watched her narrowly. 'Has he been doing something he shouldn't?'

She could feel the warmth rising under her skin, and could do nothing to stop it. She tried to laugh the moment off. 'What's that supposed to mean?'

'You know what it means, well as I do. *Something* happened 'tween you two, for sure. Think I'm dense?'

Her gaze dropped, the flush deepening. 'No,' she said huskily, 'I don't think you're dense, Jack. Just forget it, will you?'

'The bloody fool!' He said it with force. 'I thought he'd have the sense to leave you alone!'

'He did—or he would have done if I hadn't goaded him.'

'So you goaded him. Didn't have to rise to it, did he?' He studied her, the spark of anger still flickering. 'Tell me to mind my own business if you like, but he's the first to get to you, isn't he?'

Her smile came wryly. 'Was it that obvious?'

'Sure it was obvious. Why do you think Mike's been hanging round you like a randy tomcat these last few days? He was the one I'd have expected trouble from, not Ty. The man's losing his marbles!'

'He didn't realise,' she defended.

'Like hell he didn't! What are you sticking up for him for, anyway?'

She said it softly, almost to herself. 'Because I'm in love with him.'

Jack ran a distracted hand through thinning hair. 'You don't know what you're talking about, girl!'

'That's more or less what Ty said too, only you neither of you have to be right. I'm capable of knowing my own feelings.' She shook her head at the expression on his face. 'Don't look so thrown. I can't be the first to fall. He's with a woman now, isn't he?'

His eyes flickered. 'How would I know?'

'Because you know him. Probably better than anybody.' She paused, gaze appealing. 'Tell me about him, Jack.'

'That's not going to help any.'

'I don't care. I just need to know.'

The shrug was resigned. 'There isn't all that much to tell. He walked out on the family business after a row with his father ten years ago. I think he's been back a couple of times since to see his mother and sister. Like I already said, I only met him four years ago myself.'

'That's all?' Ria asked after a moment.

'All I've got. Only reason I know that much is because he let it out one night after we both got pie-eyed at a bar in Rangoon.'

'He's never said whereabouts in England he comes from?'

'No. Don't see as it matters much—unless you were thinking of looking 'em up when you get back?'

Her smile was weak. 'Hardly.'

'So?' Jack studied her questioningly. 'What do you plan on doing now?'

'The same thing I was planning on before,' she came back on as level a note as she could manage. 'Once we get to Sibu I'll be out of his hair.'

'Will he be out of yours?'

'It won't make a lot of difference. It won't be happening again.'

'Your say-so or his?'

'His, as a matter of fact. If it were up to me . . .' She left it there, biting her lip.

'Don't be a fool, girl,' Jack said gruffly. 'What you need is some young feller with a good steady job who'll give you a couple of nice kids and a regular home.'

Ria forced a laugh. 'That sounds desperately dull!'

'But safe. You'd never know where you were with a guy like Ty Morgan.'

'I'm never likely to find out.' She hesitated, searching

the worn features opposite. 'You won't say anything to him about this, will you, Jack? I can handle it.'

'Sez you.' The sideways movement of the grizzled head held a certain reluctance. 'It isn't going to be easy, but I'll keep my nose clean. Now, will you try and eat something before they come and cart you away?'

Ria complied, more to please him than from any renewal of appetite. She felt a little better for having had someone to talk to, regardless of the fact that he couldn't help. No one could help her except herself. She had to learn to live with her emotions—for the coming few days, at least.

The sun was close to setting when they reached the boat. It would be dark in less than twenty minutes. Ty was talking with a couple of Malaysian men. He broke off the conversation when he saw them approaching and came to meet them, hands thrust casually into the pockets of his khaki shorts.

'There's a festival tonight,' he announced. 'Want to stay on for it?'

'We've already eaten,' Ria told him.

'You don't have to sample the food. I thought you might like the entertainment. I made arrangements with those two over there to bring you across when you're ready. Jack will see you're all right.'

He didn't intend accompanying them himself, that was obvious. Ria shook her head, stifling the pain of it. 'I'm tired. I daresay Jack is too. It's been a long hot day.'

'O.K. Just a thought.' He sounded indifferent. 'Why don't you get in the boat while I cancel?'

Nobody spoke very much on the way back. Darkness brought a sudden squall of rain, soaking them to the skin in seconds. It had stopped again by the time they reached the *Tiger Rose*, the cloud clearing as swiftly as it had appeared. Stars sparkled like diamonds.

The deck was unlit, but Ty made no comment. It was left to Jack to berate the absent mate roundly for leaving her unattended.

'I hope you're going to give it him in the neck when

he does get back!' he added when Ty still failed to react.

'He won't be coming back,' returned the latter calmly, seizing a towel to rub vigorously at his hair. 'I paid him off.'

The older man gaped at him. 'When?'

'Before we left. He didn't lose out.'

'But why now, man?' Jack sounded bewildered. 'You have a fight or something?'

'Let's just say a difference of opinion.' Grey eyes flicked briefly in Ria's direction. 'Better get some dry clothes on. I'll make us all a drink.'

He was just as damp himself, but she refrained from pointing it out. Mike was gone. Regardless of the whys and wherefore, she could only feel relief.

She gave herself a swift rub-down in the cabin, and pulled on her jeans and other shirt. She might have to buy herself one or two extra tops, she reflected. This turn and turn about was getting to be a problem. She wished she had thought about it earlier while they had been in the town, but no doubt there would be another opportunity, either here or in Sibu. She wondered how difficult it was going to be to find another mate. Ty hadn't seemed worried by that aspect, so she could only assume he already had someone lined up. Perhaps that was what he'd been doing all day, interviewing prospects. The thought cheered her.

She had left the saloon door slightly ajar. The voices reached her before she reached it, halting her in her tracks.

'She didn't tell me,' Jack was saying. 'I guessed. You need your head seeing to, man!'

'You can't call me anything I haven't called myself,' came the heavy retort, greeted by a snort.

'Want to take a bet on it? That's no cheap little pick-up you've got back there!'

'Leave it, will you?' Ty sounded weary. 'It happened, that's all there is to it. I'll see her right.'

'Sure you will. If you really meant that you'd take her up that damned river yourself.'

The laugh was short on humour. 'Maybe I should marry her into the bargain. What's twelve years!'

'The same as it should have been last night or whenever—a hell of a sight too much. Suppose it bulled you up having a kid like that throwing herself at your head. Makes a real change from your usual line-up. God knows, you were the last thing she needed!'

'Think I don't realise it?' The shrug was almost visible. 'A bit late for being sorry, isn't it?'

There was a pause, a slight moderation of tone on Jack's part. 'So what *are* you going to do about her?'

'What I've said I'll do—find somebody to get her where she wants to go.'

'And what about getting her back again? Have you thought about *that?*'

'No, dammit, I'm trying not to.' Another pause, a sudden hard sigh. 'O.K., O.K., you made your point. I'll see to it. Just quit it for now.'

Ria leaned against the bulkhead, trying to pull herself together. She had learned nothing new. Ty might feel guilty, but that was all he felt. Well, he needn't bother. Once she got to Sibu she would be out of his hair for good. It couldn't come soon enough for her.

They left Brunei on the third morning, calling in at Miri on their way down the coast in order to satisfy the Sarawak regulations. The Rajang delta was broad and swampy, the river itself navigable by ocean-going vessels only for the first fifty miles. Jungle shrubbery crowded both banks of the swirling, muddy brown current, the trees topped by a constant fine mist as the sun drew moisture from the dripping forest.

The latter supported a wealth of wild-life, Ria knew, but there was little enough of it to be seen by the casual eye. A solitary glimpse of one of the enormous monitor lizards scavenging for fish in the shallows, a small herd of bearded pigs splashing across one of the thousand rivulets that emptied into the main flow, the occasional troop of monkeys foraging among the branches. Silent, however, it was not. The incessant buzzing of cicadas and crickets, the chorus of bird and monkey calls hypnotised the senses.

With a population of some fifty thousand or more, Sibu was larger than she had anticipated. Many were Chinese, the rest a mixture of ethnic groups with a mere scattering of European blood. For the first time she could begin to appreciate the tribal differences among these people whose skin colour ranged from dark brown through to nearly white. Shades of her father, she told herself, acknowledging the fascination. He had spent so much of his life speculating along the same lines.

'I wish I'd taken the opportunity to learn more about what he did while he was still alive,' she said wistfully to Jack as he leaned at her side watching the vendors along the wharf. 'I always used to think it was so much better to be out and doing than stuck indoors studying.'

'It still is,' he replied comfortably. 'He was one person, you're another. Wishing won't alter that.'

Ria smiled, glancing at him. 'You're a bit of a philosopher in your own way, aren't you?'

'If that's what you want to call it. I call it common sense.' He straightened, tossing his cigarette stub into the murky waters below. 'Better get back to that engine. We only made it up-river by the skin of our teeth.'

'What will happen if you can't fix it?' asked Ria. 'Can you get a new engine fitted here?'

'Doubtful.' He sounded relatively unconcerned. 'I've fixed her before, I'll fix her again. All she needs is a bit of sweet talk.'

She could do with some of that herself, thought Ria hollowly. The last few days had been among the hardest she had ever been called upon to endure. Not that Ty had been harsh with her exactly, simply aloof. She would have liked to tell him just what he could do with any plans he might be making for her benefit, but he hadn't given her the opportunity. On the odd occasions when they had found themselves alone together, his conversation had been limited to the bare essentials.

There had been no replacement for Mike. So far the two them appeared to be coping adequately alone. Where Ty intended going after leaving here she had no idea. It wasn't really important, she supposed. She would no longer be involved. All the same, they would surely need a third crew member before heading out to open sea again.

Having supervised the unloading, he had gone into the town. Ria had contemplated taking a trip in herself, but the heat was too overpowering to wander around without any special aim. She now had two spare T-shirts; there was nothing else she needed. If Ty came back with news of a guide for her, well and good. If not, she intended finding her own.

He returned around five, looking disgruntled. Luck, Ria surmised, had not been on his side. Jack's news that the engine was going to need spares not readily available in Sibu itself scarcely improved his mood.

'It's going to take at least a week to get them through,' he fumed over supper. 'If we had to get stuck anywhere I could think of a dozen better places!'

'A week should be just about time enough,' said Jack blandly. 'I can look after the boat.'

'It isn't necessary,' put in Ria hastily, sensing his drift. 'I've seen the express boats going up-river. They're always crowded with people. It isn't as if I need to trek through the jungle itself to get to Long Laha.'

'You'll be changing boats more than once, and spending nights,' rejoined Ty on a brusque note. 'You don't even speak the language.'

'Enough to get by.'

'That's a matter of opinion.' He paused a moment, then shrugged. 'I couldn't find anybody going further than Belaga, so it would probably have come to the same thing in the end. We'll leave first thing in the morning.'

All settled, his tone stated. No argument. He might

not care much for the idea himself, but that was the way it was going to be. Ria viewed the situation with mixed feelings, aware both of her heightened pulse rate and the dull heaviness in her stomach. Ty's attitude hadn't altered. He still saw her as a liability he could afford to do without. She couldn't blame him too much. What had happened between them had been as much her fault as his—perhaps even a little more. It wouldn't be happening again, that was for sure. Women were not in such short supply that he had to take any further advantage of her inexperience.

'Thanks,' she said belatedly, not bothering to conceal her own lack of enthusiasm for the prospect. 'I'll try not to be too much of a nuisance.'

She went on deck after the usual evening rain had ceased, taking advantage of the temporary lull in mosquito activity. Ty followed her up, coming to lean on the rail alongside her, a cheroot between his fingers.

'If we're going to spend a week together,' he said gruffly, 'we'd better get our priorities sorted out as of now. As far as anybody else is concerned, we're brother and sister. O.K.?'

Ria laughed shortly. 'I shouldn't think my reputation is going to suffer out here!'

His answering smile was grim. 'Mine might. One thing we're not going to need is bad blood, so if you've anything at all you want to call me get it off your chest now.'

'Why should I want to call you anything?' she asked, eyes steadfastly fixed in front of her. 'You only did what I wanted you to do. That saying, "you never miss what you've never had" isn't wholly true, you know. You completed my education. It's as simple as that.'

'I certainly did not.' The words were growled. 'A quick tumble in bed doesn't make you a woman of the world!'

'Meaning there are unscrupulous characters who might take far more advantage?' She shook her head, attempting a smile of her own. 'Forewarned is forearmed. The next man I let near me will be one I really am in love with, not just imagining myself to be.' She added wryly, 'That's terrible grammar, but you know what I mean.'

'Yes,' he said, 'I know what you mean.' His tone was dry. 'I'm glad you've had the sense to recognise it for what it was.'

'Infatuation, isn't that the word?' Ria kept her voice light. 'Don't worry, I'm over it now. I just don't want you to feel you're under any obligation because of what happened. All I wanted was to get to Sibu.'

'Having brought you this far it's up to me to see you safely through the rest,' he stated. 'With the boat laid up in dock, I shan't be losing anything. Jack can look after things while we're gone.'

Ria seized on the change of subject, unwilling to have him walk away and leave her just yet. 'What makes you and Jack so close? He's at least eighteen years older than you are.'

'Never really thought about it,' Ty admitted. 'He's been with me since I bought the *Tiger Rose*. Suppose he's almost like one of the fittings by now.'

'Chinese?' she hazarded, sidetracking again. 'The girl she was named after, I mean.'

He drew on the cheroot, emitting a fragrant cloud of smoke to keep the returning mosquitoes at bay. 'Intrigued me too at the time.'

'You didn't name her?'

'No. I knew a Tiger Lily once, never a Tiger Rose.' The half-smoked cheroot was tossed into the water below as he straightened. 'The boat leaves at seven. Better get yourself an early night. It's the last good one you're likely to see for a while.'

CHAPTER FIVE

POWERED by a huge inboard diesel engine, the boat had banquette seating down either side and a wooden roof overhead. By departure time even the latter had passengers squatting on top. Squashed between Ty and a Punan woman in a sarong supporting a bundle of miscellaneous goods in her lap, Ria could only think of the long hours ahead with trepidation.

Like Ty himself, she was wearing jeans again, which, though hot, at least afforded some protection against the insect population. The few other items they had brought along resided in the back-pack he carried.

With her head uncovered while they were under the shade of the roof, she drew some frankly curious glances from those about her. Few of them, said Ty, would have seen a European female before, much less one whose hair was shorter than any man's! Women here wore their hair long and loose and shining.

Ploughing against the current, the boat zigzagged from bank to bank of the river picking up and setting down at the various longhouses. Often there was only one building, occasionally a group of two or three together. A longhouse was just as its name suggested, built of wood planks and raised several feet from the ground to allow for flooding. The number of doors depicted the number of families sharing the semi-communal accommodation.

Children abounded, splashing and screaming in the shallows at every landing. The river was everything to everyone: road, laundry, bath, even toilet. Every community had its own dugouts from which they caught the fish that constituted a great part of their diet. Combined with the coconut palms and fruit trees surrounding each house, and small areas of cultivated land, they were almost self-sufficient.

Long Laha would be no different, Ty advised, when Ria expressed her doubts that her father could have lived in similar conditions. Just the one longhouse as far as he could remember from his fleeting glimpse of the village. Certainly facilities would be no better than these.

'It's a matter of what you're used to,' he said easily. 'Most of these people have never known anything else and can't imagine anything else, so they're not complaining. The ones who want more leave—like your father did eventually.'

'Could you?' asked Ria. 'Live like that, I mean?'

The dark head inclined. 'I could think of a lot worse. Depends on the incentive.'

No mere woman would ever tempt him that far, she thought, no matter how beautiful. He was a free spirit; he probably always would be. An assumption which brought her no particular comfort.

They reached the small township called Kapit around three o'clock in the afternoon. Ty secured two rooms in the Rajang Hotel, and left Ria there while he went to get police passes for them both to travel up-river from here to Belaga, where he would have to repeat the process. Ria was only now beginning to realise the difficulties she would have had to overcome had she been travelling alone—if she had even got this far. The Malaysian government was apparently none too keen on Europeans wandering around willy-nilly in the interior territories.

The town itself was uninspiring. Tired and aching after so many hours getting there, and with the thought of a further ten hours at least to come on the following day, Ria was only too thankful, after they had eaten, to agree to Ty's suggestion of another early night.

Despite the insect-repellent she had so lavishly applied, she was covered in mosquito bites. There were also the beginnings of a sweat rash about her waist. She applied calamine, hoping it would develop no further. Ty seemed immune to the insects: either that or they couldn't get through his toughened hide. In restrospect, the journey she had undertaken to Katmandu was starting to seem like one long picnic.

It rained on and off almost the whole of the way up to Belaga, one minute blazing sunshine, the next a solid downpour. The boat they were on today was slightly larger than the previous one, with windows instead of open sides. Even with the latter pushed as wide as they would go, the fug created by sixty or more steaming bodies was almost unbearable. The journey itself was not without its dangers, including the negotiation of a set of rapids that had Ria's heart in her mouth. It wasn't unknown, Ty admitted afterwards, for even the larger boats to swamp when the river was running high the way it was today. There was simply no alternative route for the majority of people.

Belaga was the outpost of the interior, and the home of the district officer. In actual size it wasn't much more than a large village, although it boasted a police station and a school. Housed in one vast longhouse, the Belaga bazaar was the focal point for visitors and residents alike. People met there, conducted business on the broad veranda fronting the building. Ria was fascinated to catch her first glimpse of split ears, the stretched lobes often extending as far down as the shoulder.

Ty returned from a visit to the D.O.'s office with permission to spend no more than ten days up-river. He had also exchanged the large-denomination notes Ria was carrying for a stack of smaller value in Brunei dollars.

'You'll not be able to get all this lot in that pocket of yours,' he pointed out. 'You'll have to let me carry it for you.'

'I trust you,' she said lightly, and saw his mouth twist.

'It'll be safer than it's been at any time since you left England. Have you any idea of the risk you've been taking?'

Blue eyes met grey, refusing to flinch away. 'I survived.'

'More by good luck that good management. Anyway, I'll hang on to it till we find who we're looking for—*if* we do.'

Ria's brows drew together. 'You really think there's a doubt?'

'There has to be some. Anything might have happened in five years. She could have moved to another village. It happens. If she's made a new life for herself she might not welcome any reminder.'

'She already has a reminder,' Ria pointed out. 'Her son will be almost five years old. Dad said he was fair-haired and fair-skinned like him, and quite European in feature—so far as one can tell with a small baby.'

'If he survived. The mortality rate gets higher the further in you go. There's a flying doctor service, but the visits aren't all that frequent.' A smile touched his lips. 'Still, if he grew up with even a fraction of his half-sister's spirit he'll have stood a good chance.'

She said softly, 'Do I take that as a compliment?'

'It was meant as one.' His regard was centred on her face. 'I never knew any other girl—or woman either, if it comes to that—who could have taken what you're taking this trip without coming apart at the seams. It's going to get a lot worse, you realise?'

They were seated in one of the Chinese coffee-shops close by the wharf. Outside it was already dark, the air dank with the smell of rotting vegetation. The river was running high and fast, swirling around the log-landing stage with a greedy sucking sound. Thunder rolled in the distance.

'I never expected it to be easy,' Ria said. 'Although if this is the dry season, I'd hate to experience the wet!'

Ty laughed. 'We're between monsoons. Give it another month or so.'

In another month or so she would be home and dry, in more ways than the one. Her throat felt tight. She said thickly, 'Where are we staying tonight? There don't appear to be any hotels, as such.'

'We've been invited to the home of one of the officials.'

'Someone you know?'

'Not up to an hour ago. I had to do a lot of persuading to get those passes, but we finished up friends. His name is Rahim. He's a Kenyan by birth, educated in Kuching. That makes him one of an élite.'

'And he thinks I'm your sister?'

'No.' The smile held self-mockery. 'I had to show both our passports. I told him the whole story, up to a point. He remembers your father coming through, although he wasn't aware of any marriage having taken place.'

Ria looked at him sharply. 'You're suggesting it might not have been official?'

'Would it make any difference?'

She thought about it for a moment. 'No,' she said at length with conviction.

Ty shrugged. 'Well, whatever, Rahim respects your motives in wanting to find the woman yourself, even though by rights he shouldn't allow it to happen. He's eager to meet you. I said we'd be there for the evening meal, so if you've finished we'll get going. Give ourselves time to get cleaned up before we eat.'

Rahim turned out to be man perhaps in his late thirties. Small of stature, and very light-skinned, he lived alone except for one woman who came daily to clean and cook. He spoke excellent English. Once the initial greetings were done with, he wasted no time in showing them where they were to sleep that night. The single-storey house had a broad, covered veranda running round all four sides. Part of this had been partitioned off from the rest, and provided with a couple of camp beds complete with mosquito nets. Right next door to this extra room had been rigged a primitive shower.

'Not luxurious, I'm afraid,' apologised their host, mistaking Ria's silence, 'but clean and quite comfort-able. The water in the shower tank is warm if you would care to use it.' He smiled. 'One of the things I missed the most when I first came up from the coast.'

Ria said quickly, 'You're very kind. Thank you. A shower will be wonderful.'

She met Ty's glance as the other man withdrew, unable to resist the faint sarcasm. 'I thought you'd made the relationship clear?'

'I imagine this is the only spare room in the house,' he returned, seemingly unperturbed. 'We're not being asked to share a bed. Do you want first go in the shower or shall I?'

'You go,' she invited.

Clean towels had been left ready for them on the nearest bed. Dropping the back-pack in a corner, he went out via the flimsy rattan door. Bare moments later there was a metallic pumping sound, followed by the splashing of water.

Ria extracted a clean shirt and briefs from the pack, and sat down gingerly on the edge of a bed to wait her turn. Ty might be taking this turn of events in his stride, but she had been unprepared. Last night, knowing that only a thin wall lay between then, sleep had been hard enough to come by. Tonight would be worse. If only she could persuade him to forget about her age and lack of experience. She wouldn't ask him for anything; she wouldn't expect anything. All she wanted was to be in his arms again, to feel his lips, his hands, the racing of her blood. It was racing now at the very thought.

He was wearing nothing but the towel slung about lean hips when he came back to the room.

'It's all yours,' he said briefly. 'I'll go on through to join Rahim as soon as I'm ready.'

The shower was housed in a small cubicle, the water allowed to drain away beneath the house via a hole cut in the roughly tiled floor. A little more damp hardly mattered in this climate, Ria supposed. Primitive though it might be, it was still adequate to do the job. She washed her hair too while she was under the flow. Even in the relatively short time since it had last been cut, it had grown considerably, the ends starting to curl with a will of their own. For the first time in years she had no desire to start hacking at it again. The tomboy stage was behind her. From now on she would stop fighting her femininity. She wondered if Ty might notice any difference.

Clean or not, she was growing tired of donning the same old things. Her shorts were little protection against the marauding livestock, but they were at least cool and comfortable. She only hoped they would be regarded as suitable dinner wear. There was no mirror available, and she carried none of her own. She had never, she acknowledged wryly, even thought about it in the past. Not much point, anyway, when the only thing she could do was criticise her appearance. Regardless of what Jack had said, it would take far more than longer hair and a dress to transform her.

Dinner was simple but filling: chicken cooked in a tasty if rather hot sauce and served with quantities of rice and boiled pumpkin, followed by fresh fruit.

'If I'd known you were coming,' Rahim apologised, 'I would have ordered something better.'

'When you're used to living out of tins, this couldn't *be* better,' Ty responded, helping himself to more of the sauce. 'We're grateful for the hospitality. The rest-house was full. You must have seen some changes here in seven years.'

The Malaysian smiled. 'Some good, some bad. We survive.' His eyes moved to Ria. 'Your father would have deplored the loss of so much of our native culture.'

'You knew him well?' she asked eagerly.

He shook his head. 'I met him only twice, once when he was on his way up-river and again when he returned many months later.' He paused before adding succinctly, 'I knew of no marriage.'

'Is it against the law for a European to marry a tribal woman?'

'Discouraged would be closer. News travels fast both

up and down the river. I can't believe such a marriage
could have taken place without some rumour filtering
through.'

'It did,' she stated flatly. 'He was quite definite on
that point. I imagine he might not have felt quite so
guilty about deserting her if she'd only been his
common law wife.'

Rahim looked puzzled. 'Common law?'

'Where two people live together without any official
ceremony.' Ty lifted broad shoulders. 'It isn't all that
important, is it? She's still entitled to the money he left
her.'

'Of course. And I'm sure it will be gratefully received.
Such a sum would enable her to move down-river here
to Belaga if she wishes—perhaps even to set up a small
business. You said she was educated.'

'My father said she was.' Ria added curiously, 'Are
all children offered the same opportunity?'

'If they want it, and if the parents can manage
without their help in day-to-day living. They have to be
boarded here in Belaga. Most longhouses are too far for
a daily journey. Other districts have their own centres.'

'And no sex discrimination?'

Rahim looked surprised. 'There are girls as well as
boys in the schools, but only by their own choice.'

'English women are militant for equal rights,' put in
Ty sardonically. 'Most of them don't know when
they're well off.'

From the expression on Rahim's face it was as clear
as mud. Wisely he shelved the subject. 'Your boat
leaves at six o'clock,' he said. 'It will take you two,
perhaps even three days to reach Long Laha, depending
on how the river is running. There has been more rain
than is normal for this time of year. Remember that ten
days is the absolute maximum you can be permitted to
extend your stay.' He smiled again, wryly this time. 'As
it is, I'll have to answer to my superior when he returns
from his tour for allowing you even that much.'

'We'll be back inside the week,' promised Ty before

Ria could speak. 'If we haven't found her by then we never will.'

The woman who had cooked the meal had left the house by the time they finished eating. Rahim made coffee himself, bringing it out to the veranda where his guests were catching the fitful breeze. The thunder was still rolling around the hills, with the occasional flicker of lightening across the distant skyline. Cicadas competed with loudly croaking frogs.

Even at night the heat scarcely diminished, heavy and sultry like an all-enveloping cloak. Mosquitoes formed a regular cloud about the two pressure lamps. Ria had given up trying to repel them, and seemed to be faring the better for it. The heat rash about her waist was something else. She could feel her shirt sticking to it every time she moved.

Weariness clouded her mind, fading the two male voices to a pleasant distance. She began to drift, living afresh the journey she had made so far. England seemed a long, long time ago—another life. She had experienced the same feelings last year in Nepal, or very nearly the same. Readjustment had been difficult enough then, heaven only knew what it was going to be like this time. She didn't want to go back. Not now, not ever. Life out here might not be easy, but it had some purpose. To sail the South China seas with Ty would be the ultimate bliss. He wouldn't have to marry her; she'd be content simply to be his woman. She wouldn't even object to the name of the boat. *Tiger Rose.* It conjured up an image of oriental beauty. Perhaps he had been telling the truth when he denied all knowledge of its origin, perhaps not. If it was in the past it shouldn't matter. The present was her concern.

'Why don't you go to bed if you're tired?' suggested the subject of her thoughts, jerking her back to reality again. 'I shan't be long myself.'

Blue eyes met grey, the latter too enigmatic to read with any accuracy. 'I think I will,' Ria said lamely. She pushed herself to her feet, looking at their host. 'Thank you again for your hospitality. I can't tell you how much it's appreciated.'

'It's been my pleasure,' he said formally. 'You must stay with me again on your way back to the coast.'

No more than a week from now, Ty had said. That was longer than he had first allowed. If they didn't find Jemo it wouldn't be for want of trying. What she would do with the money if they failed she hadn't begun to consider yet. Ria supposed, as next of kin, it would rightfully be hers, but the thought held few attractions. No use trying to cross bridges before she came to them, anyhow. Time would tell.

She was in bed but still awake when Ty eventually came through. She lay listening to the sounds he made undressing, heard the protesting creak of the camp bed as he slid his length into it, then a heavy sigh as he settled himself for sleep. He carried no night attire in the pack, she knew. Protected by the mosquito net draped from a ring in the roof, she was naked herself beneath the single sheet. Her body shook with tremors, every nerve and sinew stretched taut. He had to come to her; she couldn't go to him. Please God, make him come!

'Stop holding your breath and get to sleep,' he said brusquely into the silence. 'We've a long way to go yet.'

She did sleep eventually, wakening again in the small hours to a raw discomfort. Some of the small water blisters formed about her waist must have burst, she realised, feeling the sticky wetness beneath her. The calamine was a must if she wasn't to finish up with an infection. The problem was how to reach it without wakening Ty.

He opened his eyes the moment she stirred, coming up on an elbow to look across at her.

'Something wrong?'

'I'm all right,' she said. 'Just a bit of a rash. I thought I might put some calamine on it.'

'Stay where you are,' he ordered, throwing back the sheet and lifting the net. 'I'll get it.'

He was still wearing his dark blue underpants, Ria saw, as he crossed to where he had left the back-pack. Heart thudding, she watched him extract the bottle and tear a piece from the small pack of cotton wool.

'I can manage,' she said when he came over to where she lay. 'Just leave them on the floor.'

'And have every bug in town paying a visit?' with irony. 'Turn over and let me have a look.'

Ria did so, steeling herself for the touch of his fingers against her bare skin as he drew down the sheet. A low whistle escaped his lips as he viewed the damage.

'That must be giving you gyp!' he declared. 'How long have you had it?'

'Since yesterday.' Her voice was muffled. 'My waistband must have rubbed. I think I might have to wear shorts tomorrow as well and let the mosquitoes do their worst!'

'You're going to need something loose to let the air get to this.' He was bending over her, patting on the cooling liquid with a gentleness she found infinitely disturbing. 'How far round does it go?'

'Almost the whole way,' she acknowledged. 'I can cope with the front myself.'

'I might as well finish the job while I'm about it,' he said without inflection. 'You don't have anything I haven't already seen. You'd better sit up until the back is dry.'

Ria obeyed slowly and with some reluctance, steeling herself against the ridiculous urge to cover her breasts with her hands. The pain from the rash was as nothing compared with the turmoil inside her as Ty bent his head to his task. She wanted so badly to touch him, to stroke her fingers over the dark crispness of his hair, to feel the tensing of muscle in the broad shoulders, the swelling of biceps, the hardness of his chest. Her breathing roughened to the memory of how it had been before—the crushing, yet somehow so supportable, weight of him, the taste of his lips on hers, the sense of possession and of being possessed. Whatever the

emotion he aroused in her might be called, it was
overwhelming in its power.

'Stop trembling,' he said gruffly, recapping the bottle.
'You're not helping at all.'

'I can't help it,' she whispered. 'I really can't, Ty! I
want you so much.'

He groaned suddenly. 'How many times do I have to
tell you you're not supposed to make the running that
way? I'm not cut out for turning the other cheek.'

'Then don't,' she invited. 'Make love to me again. I
shan't expect anything else from you once all this is
over.'

The skin around his mouth whitened from the sheer
pressure as his teeth clamped together. 'I made myself a
promise,' he forced out, 'and for once in my damned
life, I'm going to keep it! Go back to sleep.'

Shame swamped her as he pushed himself to his feet
and went to put the bottle back in the pack. She had
thrown herself at his head and been rejected. Could
anything be more degrading than that?

Easing herself back beneath the sheet, she turned
on her side away from the other bed. The calamine
had cooled the burning in her skin, but it could do
nothing for the heat still inside her. She felt consumed
by it.

The ancient, metal-hulled river boat was crewed by
several Chinese. With the rickety cabin full of trade
goods, the only place for passengers was out in the full
heat of the sun. Ty purchased an umbrella from one of
the vendors, and insisted Ria use it for protection from
time to time. He was used to it, he said; she wasn't. The
last thing they needed was a case of sunstroke.

Rahim had managed to procure her a sarong in
mingled blue and brown cotton. Worn with one of her
own short-sleeved shirts and a pair of canvas sandals, it
created an outfit that was both comfortable and
practical. After the first half-hour or so, Ria forgot her
initial reticence in the relief afforded by the lack of

pressure at her waistline. The rash was responding to the calamine, but needed a day or two to heal properly.

It was a long day, with only the occasional stretch of rapids to break the monotony. In a boat the size of this one, even the latter meant no more than a temporary discomfort. Portions from a huge pan of cooked rice mixed with salted fish could be purchased when required. Ria couldn't face it and settled for fruit instead, but Ty consumed several platefuls and even appeared to enjoy it.

They stopped for the night at a forty-door longhouse where all passengers shared the one room, with no concessions made towards separating the sexes. The term 'room' was in itself a misnomer, as in all the vast building partitions between families consisted at the most of a woven rattan screen. Everyone from the boat slept on thin mats without bothering to undress.

Surprisingly, Ria found little difficulty in getting to sleep herself after the communal meal, coming awake at first light along with the rest of the ongoing passengers to partake of a light breakfast of maize cakes and fruit before setting forth again on the water. Whatever curiosity Ty's and her presence on board the boat might have first engendered, it had all but disappeared. They were accepted, treated as friends. None of their fellow passengers was going to Long Laha, although two were heading beyond to Long Busang. Questioned by Ty, they denied any knowledge of a Ukit woman named Jemo, which Ria found depressing. If she had moved on there was going to be little time left to try tracing her.

They reached their destination around lunchtime on the third day, dropped off with a firm promise from the Chinese crew to call for them in two days' time on their return down-river. Long Laha was a thirty-door longhouse, at present fully occupied to judge from the number of people spread around the *kampong*. The Ukit race was pale-skinned, the women in particular delicate of feature. Few of the latter bothered to wear anything at all above the waist.

Surrounded by loudly chattering children, they were taken to pay their respects to the *penghulu* of the village. He received them in a corner of the wide veranda fronting the longhouse, a small, dignified man with a wrinkled, aged face and a voice devoid of any aggression. He spoke no English himself but appeared to have no difficulty in understanding Ty's explanation in Malay of why they were here, his gaze shifting to scan Ria's features almost as if in recognition. One of the youths nearby was summoned with a flick of a finger, to be despatched again with a bare few words.

'She's here,' said Ty, glancing in Ria's direction. 'They're fetching her in from the *padi*-field now. The boy is around somewhere. In the meantime, we're invited to lunch. It's an honour to eat with the *penghulu*, so make the most of it.'

At that moment there was nothing Ria would have liked better than to be shown a place where she could wash, but it would have been impolite to say so. Now that the time was at last on her, the thought of meeting her stepmother was daunting. What would they say to each other? How would Jemo be likely to feel about the daughter of the man who had deserted her? Educated or not, she was from a different world.

CHAPTER SIX

THE meal was served and eaten on the veranda, the inevitable rice accompanied by scrambled egg mixed with boiled onion, and quantities of an edible fern. For dessert there were various kinds of fruit, followed by coffee served in ornate and obviously cherished earthenware cups.

Ria ate everything offered her but tasted little. The *padi*-fields couldn't be so far away from the village. Jemo should have been here by now. Perhaps she had refused to see her visitors. She could hardly be blamed for taking that attitude. However, the *kampong* was too confined for her go on avoiding them for long.

Only when the *penghulu* made a signal after they had finished coffee did Ria realise that the meeting had been deliberately delayed until the meal was finished. The woman who answered his summons was no more than twenty-two or -three years of age, her long black hair tied back from a face that showed little expression. Her father hadn't exaggerated, thought Ria fleetingly. Jemo was beautiful. She was very light-skinned, but the boy clinging shyly to her side was lighter still, the fair curls covering his head so like Ria's own she could only stare at him in shock. She got awkwardly to her feet, not sure what kind of greeting she should offer.

'I'm Ria Brownlow,' she said hesitantly. 'Perhaps my father . . .'

'Hugh spoke of you when he was here,' replied the other, coming to her aid. Her voice was serene, her English easily understandable. 'Was he afraid to come himself?'

Ria bit her lip. There was only one way to tell it and that was straight out. 'I'm afraid my father died several weeks ago,' she said quietly. 'I only learned about you and Tamo just before it happened. He asked me to tell you he was sorry.'

The other girl's head had bowed for a moment, but her recovery was swift. 'You're very welcome,' she said. Her glance flickered towards Ty. 'This is your husband?'

'No.' Ria performed hasty introductions. 'He helped me get here,' she finished. 'I couldn't have done it without him.' She smiled at the boy who was beginning to take an interest in proceedings. 'Does your son speak any English?'

'No more than a few words,' came the reply. 'He has yet to begin his lessons. In another year or two he'll go to Belaga to receive schooling, and then we'll see.' Her hand caressed the fair head as she spoke, dark eyes glancing proudly downwards. 'If you've finished eating, perhaps we may talk together?'

'You go ahead,' said Ty as Ria looked his way. 'I'll have some more coffee.'

Jemo led the way along the veranda, choosing a door close to the far end and ushering Ria through into the shadowed space beyond. Mats woven from split bamboo covered both the wooden floor and the raised platform built along the rear wall. Apart from a semi-solid screen of shelving bearing a variety of personal goods, there was no furniture. Cooking, Ria already knew, was a communal affair performed in one section of the two-hundred-and-fifty foot building.

Shaded or not, it was oppressively hot inside. Feeling the perspiration springing from her scalp, Ria could only envy her hostess's apparent immunity. She joined Jemo cross-legged on the mat, hoping her stamina would be equal to any demands made on it. There was so much to talk about, so much to learn.

Tamo had been despatched to play with the other children. Even so, there was little privacy in which to conduct a conversation. Voices echoed from all parts of the vast structure.

'You're wondering how a man such as your father

was could have lived this way for any length of time?'
suggested Jemo with perception, watching Ria's face.
'Perhaps I had the medicine man make up a spell for
him.' Her smile made mock of the words. 'Yet he was
happy here for almost a year following his studies. He
liked, he used to say, the utter simplicity of our life.
Down-river they are attempting to modernise our
longhouses, but here we are left to follow our
traditional paths. For how long, no one knows.'

'Did you ever go any further than Belaga?' asked Ria
curiously, unable to believe that anyone who spoke and
thought like this young woman could possibly be
content to live such a primitive lifestyle. 'I know you
were at school there.'

'For three years only. I couldn't be spared any longer
than that.'

'But your English is so good!'

'Much of it I learned from Hugh, although I have
little opportunity to practise. Many of our people speak
your language to some degree, but few here in Long
Laha itself. My family know a few words between
them.'

'You share this room with them?'

Jemo inclined her head. 'With my parents, my two
brothers and one sister. When Hugh was here we built a
room of our own, but I couldn't stay there alone.' Her
gaze was very level. 'Now that I know he will never
come back, I can, as he would have said, get on with
my life.'

Ria said softly, 'You'll marry again?'

'Perhaps. But only with a man who will agree to let
Tamo attend school for the full nine years. The
government will pay for him to live at the hostel in
Balaga during each term, and the schooling itself is free,
so there is nothing to stop him.'

'But you'll still need money to give him the other
things he needs?'

Jemo smiled faintly. 'Money is always useful, but not
essential. We trade our rattan baskets and mats for any

goods we need. They fetch a high price at the coast it seems.'

'I see.' Ria was nonplussed. She had made this journey in the belief that she was bringing aid, only to find that far from being deprived, Jemo actually wanted for nothing. Not the whole point of the exercise, though, she reminded herself. She had kept her promise to her father. That was what counted. As for the money, well, Jemo must do with it as she thought fit.

She imparted the news in as businesslike a manner as she could manage, seeing the dark eyes widen when she named the sum available in Brunei dollars.

'You have to take it,' she finished. 'It was what Dad wanted.'

'Of course I'll take it.' Jemo obviously suffered from no false pride. 'I said money wasn't essential, but there are many extras it will buy. You have enough left to get home again?'

'I already have my ticket from Singapore,' Ria agreed.

'That's a long distance from Borneo.'

'Ty will get me there.'

'Ah, yes.' The smile widened. 'Your man.'

I wish he was, it was on the tip of Ria's tongue to say, but she refrained. 'Just a good friend,' she said instead, and knew she wasn't believed for a moment. She moved restlessly. 'Is there anywhere I can bathe safely? It's so hot in here.'

'Of course.' Jemo got lightly to her feet. 'I'll show you.'

Along with several of the village men, Ty was sitting around drinking the milky-coloured liquor made from fermented rice when Ria went to fetch towel and soap from the pack. He seemed to have made a friend of the *penghulu*, who was providing the beverage.

'Just watch it,' he advised on hearing where she was going. 'We don't want you feeding the crocs!'

'There are no crocodiles in this part of the river,' said Jemo reassuringly as the two of them left the party to it.

'Also, the women use the small river for washing because it is cleaner.'

It was indeed. Running only a short distance from the *kampong*, the tributary wound between rocky shores, forming a pool deep enough for diving at the point to which Jemo led the way. The water was sparklingly clear and quite free of debris. Ria could hardly wait to get in.

'You're not staying?' she asked as the other turned away.

Jemo shook her head. 'It's my turn to work in the *padi*-field, but I'll see you again tonight. No one will disturb you here.'

Ria hoped not. It was good to be alone for a while. Stripping off her clothing, she poised herself on the edge for a brief moment savouring the anticipation of what was to come before diving cleanly into the water. The coolness was wonderful, an instant refreshment. Surfacing, she shook the moisture from her hair and swam back to fetch her soap from the bank. Wash first, then play. She was going to make the most of this delight.

Half an hour passed before she knew it. With the sunlight angling through the trees, and just the cicadas and the frogs for company, it was so beautifully peaceful. Here in the water she was safe from the mosquitoes and sandflies, although keeping a sharp look-out for snakes. The rash about her waist had all but disappeared, leaving her skin smooth and unmarred. She'd been lucky, she knew. An infection could have been disastrous.

Risking the insect attack, she hauled herself at length on to a large flat rock in the middle of the river, standing up and smoothing moisture from her hair as she surveyed the scene. Small, brilliantly coloured kingfishers darted and skimmed across the surface of the water, ignoring her presence in their endless quest for food. It was difficult to believe that she was actually in the middle of one of the wildest tracts of jungle still left on earth. Her father had loved this place. She could understand why. Yet she could also understand how he had eventually found it too confining. What she had to condemn was the fact that he had left both Jemo and his son to live out their lives in this same confinement. The former was intelligent. She would have adapted readily enough to the world outside—had she been given the chance.

Some instinct jerked her from her thoughts, the hair prickling along the nape of her neck. When she looked up Ty was standing on the bank watching her. He had a cheroot between his fingers, the tip smouldering. His eyes were narrowed, the muscles in his neck tensed. How long he had been there she had no way of knowing. It scarcely mattered.

For a long moment their gazes clashed and held. Ty was the first to make a move, throwing down the cheroot and grinding it out beneath his boot heel with a certain deliberation. Ria stood motionless as he took off his clothes, oblivious to everything but the knowledge of what was to happen.

He entered the water cleanly, surfacing right in front of the rock to haul himself to her side. There was plenty of room for two providing they stood close. Ty made sure they did, his hands lifting her, capturing her, his mouth claiming its rights. Ria gave willingly, the passion flaring inside her a match for his own. She loved him so much, this man of hers. And he was hers. There was no doubting it now. Nothing mattered except being together.

They made love right there on the rock with the water swirling past, the sound of it like music in Ria's ears. When he came into her she cried out, not in pain this time but in sheer ecstasy because it was what her body had craved for so long. He filled her, completed her, gave her a reason for living. There would never be anyone else but Ty, she thought blindly in that final moment before the world split apart.

It was Ty who drew her into the water, finding a foothold to support himself while he held her securely against the rippling flow. There was a certain wry acceptance in the tilt of his lips. 'You've got me hogtied, you little witch,' he stated. 'I can no more leave you alone than fly!'

'I'm glad.' She was exultant, tasting power for the first time in her life. 'I don't want you to leave me alone, Ty. I want to make love until we're both drained!'

'Yes, well, the way you're behaving that might not take very long. Only now we're getting out of this river before something nasty comes swimming by.' He kissed her fleetingly on the lips and turned her round, pushing her shorewards. 'Go on.'

She reached the bank ahead of him, dragging herself from the water to seize her towel.

'You didn't bring one?' she asked as Ty joined her.

'I came looking for you because you'd been gone so long, not because I felt like a swim,' he acknowledged, stretching out. 'I'll borrow that when you've finished.'

Ria said softly. 'Sorry if I worried you.'

'No, you're not. You stayed down here purposely so I'd have to come and find you.'

Had she? Ria wondered. The time had gone so fast. Not that it mattered either way. He had come, that was all she cared about. She gave him a sideways glance, feeling her stomach muscles tighten afresh. He was magnificent—like a Greek statue! No other man could match him—and not just physically either. Two weeks ago she hadn't even known what wanting a man was like, outside books and films. She could only marvel at the difference in her outlook.

Ty shot out a sudden arm, catching her by the ankle and pulling her down across him. His eyes glinted at her, mouth wickedly curved. 'You were saying back there?'

Her insides melted, fused, her whole mind focused on the exquisite sensation as they came together again. There was no future, no past, only the present—and it was beyond all imagining.

*　　*　　*

Sunset was already close when they finally made their way back to the *kampong*. Jemo had returned from the *padi*-field. She greeted them with her usual serenity, but there was a knowledgeable gleam in her eye.

'You are to share a room in the *penghulu*'s quarters,' she announced. 'That will be satisfactory?'

'Quite,' Ty agreed drily. 'Tell him we're honoured.'

'Tonight,' Jemo continued, 'there is to be a feast in celebration of your arrival. Already the women are preparing the food.'

'I can manage a clean top,' said Ria regretfully, 'but I'm afraid I don't have another sarong. Will shorts be frowned on, do you think?'

'I can give you a sarong to wear,' offered the Malaysian girl. 'I have several. I'll fetch one now.'

The *penghulu* owned a whole suite of rooms in which he housed a large and still expanding family. Guests were allocated space of their own, although the privacy afforded was minimal. Noise bombarded the ears from all directions: the grunting and snorting of the village pigs herded in pens beneath the longhouse, barking dogs, the thudding of drums and resounding boom of metal gongs as the 'band' began getting into the mood. And rising above all, the sound of voices, mostly male, Ria noted.

'Dad must have been deaf to stand this racket for all those months,' she commented cheerfully to Ty as she donned the silky sarong Jemo had provided. 'Although I suppose you'd get used to it eventually.'

'You can get used to anything,' he agreed, then gave vent to a muttered curse as the razor he was using drew blood under his jawline. 'I should have settled for growing a beard on this trip,' he added roughly. 'Either that or kept off the damned *borak*. The stuff's lethal!'

Ria dropped to her knees at his side, hearing the sudden sharp intake of his breath as she leaned forward impulsively to lick the bright droplet from his skin with the tip of her tongue. 'I like you cleanshaven,' she murmured.

'You wouldn't know the difference,' he growled. 'You didn't know much about anything before I got to you.'

She was so close to him she could see her own reflection in the grey eyes against the soft glow of the oil lamp. The expression in them was difficult to define with any accuracy. 'Do you regret it?' she whispered.

There was cynicism in his faint smile. 'Yes, I regret it. Not that it alters a damned thing.'

'I'm glad.' She slid her arms about his neck and kissed him on the lips, using every artifice she had learned during those hours they had spent at the river to reach him. He pulled her down across him, holding her head steady beneath his with one hand while the other sought one small, firm breast. His palm felt slightly rough against the softer skin, but all the more stimulating for it.

'I wish they were bigger for you,' she whispered against his mouth.

'They're perfect the way they are,' he returned gruffly. 'Every inch of you is perfect!' He bent his head to find her nipple with his tongue, teasing it for a brief, aching moment before putting her reluctantly from him. 'Later, when there's more time. As guests of honour, we can't be late for the festivities.'

Roofed over, and several yards wide, the veranda formed a fine communal meeting place. Jemo introduced her parents, who appeared to bear no grudge against the man who had deserted their daughter. Chunks of sizzling pork served on beds of rice formed the main dish of the evening, accompanied by other, unidentifiable meats, maize cakes and unlimited fruit. *Borak* flowed like water. Ria tried a little for herself, finding it gritty between her teeth and searing in its effect. She left it alone after that, wondering how Ty and the other men could toss back whole cupfuls of the stuff without burning out their stomachs in the process.

From a steady start, the drummers gradually hotted

up their tempo until the very air trembled to the beat. Only then did the dancing begin, first one young virile male springing to his feet to perform a series of wild gyrations, then another, their individual performances watched with critical eyes and loudly commented upon. When the girls danced they did it together in one long line, bodies moving in supple, sinuous rhythm, skin gleaming like oiled silk in the lamplight, every gesture and glance a deliberate provocation to the watching men. As the evening progressed, couples began to pair off, vanishing into the darkness outside with no attempt made to conceal their intention.

'Trial marriages,' said Ty, sensing Ria's interest. 'Virginity doesn't last long here either.'

There was too much noise going on around them for anyone to overhear what they were saying. Ria had to lean close to hear the words herself. 'Mine lasted as long as I wanted it to,' she stated firmly. 'And I bet I'm a lot older than most of the girls here, too!'

His smile was cynical. 'In years, maybe, the rest I wouldn't be sure.'

Ria laughed, refusing to be put down. 'That might have been true when I first set out on this trip, but I've learned an awful lot since!'

'Have you?' He sounded suddenly grim. 'I wonder?'

His mood had changed; Ria wasn't sure why. The *borak* he had drunk could be acting as a depressive, she supposed, although he showed little outward sign of inebriation. She wished he would sweep her up and out into the darkness, the way so many others had gone already. Making love was as vital to these people as it was becoming to her—except that she already knew which man above all others she wanted to be with.

The crowd was thinning out. Jemo herself was no longer to be seen. Like so many other of his fellow men, the *penghulu* had fallen asleep—or passed out—snoring away happily on the mat where he had been sitting. No one took the slightest notice. In all probability they would stay there all night.

Swept by longing, Ria brushed her cheek against Ty's sleeve. 'Take me to bed,' she pleaded.

'Wait till you're asked,' came the prompt reply, but there was no anger in it. One hand came up to stroke over her hair, lingering for a brief moment on the vulnerable nape of her neck. She felt his sigh rise from somewhere down deep. 'Let's go then,' he said.

It was hot and airless in the room, but she didn't care. The taste of salt on his skin simply added to her pleasure. She gave herself to him with total abandonment, moaning her need of him, writhing like a wild thing in his arms until he lost all control himself and took her the way she wanted to be taken: fiercely, possessively, as a full-grown woman not an untried girl.

Later, listening to the sound of his breathing as he slept, she knew she could never be more content than she was at this moment. Whatever happened, they couldn't be parted. They meant too much to each other now.

Including those whose hangovers still hung over, the whole community set out on a fishing trip next morning. Ria was happy to accompany them. She was happy to do anything providing Ty was there too.

Taking every available boat loaded with nets, and food left over from the night before, they set off en masse up the minor river, dragging the boats where the water became shallow while the children ran splashing and screaming ahead. Tamo was as boisterous as the next when let loose, Ria was glad to note, his fair head catching the dappled sunlight as he ran in the midst of the throng. He might carry some of her father's genes, but that was all. Environment formed character: Tamo was a Ukit through and through, and accepted as such. Whether he would experience the same acceptance if and when he widened his horizons was something she couldn't afford to worry about too much. His mother held sole responsibility when it came to looking after his interests.

The fishing commenced in a wide pool a couple of

miles upstream after nets had been strung across
suitably narrow points on the way. Poison made from
powdered tuba root was used to bring the fish to the
surface, where everyone joined in the rush to net or
spear as many as possible, getting in each other's way
and yelling with excitement as the tally began to rise.
Ria kept out of it, content to watch from the bank
while Ty waded in with the rest, a trident in his hands.
Sporting it wasn't, but with so many to feed there was
little time, she supposed, for the niceties.

Gradually they worked their way downstream, driving
any escapees before them into the nets. Fires were lit and
some of the catch barbecued and eaten on the spot. The
rest would later be smoked for keeping, said Jemo, who
had seated herself at Ria's side during the meal. Mixed
with rice, it was considered a great delicacy.

'Your father liked to fish,' she added. 'But he would
use a rod and line and throw back the little ones.' Her
smile was reminiscent. 'He was a kind man.'

'Did you love him?' asked Ria quietly, aware that Ty
was deep in conversation with the *penghulu*. 'Really love
him, I mean?'

'For what other reason would I have married a white
man?' came the equable response. 'We spent much time
together when he was recovering from his sickness. We
both of us grew to love.' She paused, eyes shadowed a
little. 'The marriage was by tribal ceremony only. It
would not have been counted as lawful by the
government. By going away he divorced me—that is
also one of our customs.'

'So you could have married again at any time?'

'Yes.' The sigh was heavy. 'There have been other
men who wanted me for a wife, but hope lives long. I
am grateful that you came to tell me the truth.'

'He was so much older than you,' Ria couldn't help
saying. 'At least twenty-five years.'

'Years are not important,' Jemo replied. 'It is what a
man is that matters. Your Ty is no youth, and he has
experienced much, but you love him still.'

Ria's smile was wry. 'Do I make it that obvious?'

'Why should you not?' Jemo sounded surprised. 'You are his woman.'

His woman, but was he really her man? wondered Ria with a sudden swing towards depression. Time alone would tell.

The boat arrived mid-morning to pick the two of them up. Everyone came down to the river to see them off, some taking advantage of the moment to trade with the crew. Saying goodbye to Jemo and her son was one of the hardest things Ria had ever done.

'I'll be back,' she promised. 'One day I'll come again.'

'You shouldn't make promises you can't keep,' said Ty brusquely when the waving villagers were lost to sight around the first bend in the river. 'You did what you were asked to do, now forget it.'

Ria stole a glance at him, conscious of the other passengers watching the two of them with unconcealed curiosity. He had been in an odd mood since wakening—not at all like the man with whom she had gone to sleep. They had been so close, so very, very close. Why he'd changed she had no clear idea. Now was not the time to be asking pertinent questions, she acknowledged. They would have to wait. Perhaps the *borak* was to blame, although he had drunk relatively little of it last night.

The day wore on, hot, steamy and uncomfortable. Shaded by the umbrella, Ria dozed from time to time, using Ty's shoulder as a pillow. He made no attempt to put an arm about her, his whole body stiff and unyielding. Sick with a growing fear, she tried to reassure herself that everything would be all right once they got back to Belaga where they could be alone again. It had to be all right. What they had shared this past two days and nights was too precious to be lost.

Travelling with the flow instead of against it, they made better time on the downward journey, arriving in Belaga on the evening of the second day. Rahim greeted them with a pleasure mingled with relief. He could still be in trouble for allowing them to travel into the interior at all, but at least they had returned well within the stated time.

Eating was the last thing Ria felt like doing, but she was forced to make some show. Rahim refused to take the sarong back, saying she should keep it as a souvenir of her visit. Eventually she left the two men talking and went to bed, too troubled in her mind to sleep. Lying there, waiting for Ty to come, she wished with desperation that they were back in the jungle. Everything had been so simple there. Belaga was only on the fringes of civilisation but it exerted an influence. Her own emotions were no longer quite so clear-cut any more.

He came at last, treading quietly so as not to disturb her. Ria waited until he was undressed and actually getting into the other bed before taking her courage in both hands.

'What did I do?' she asked.

There was silence for a moment. She could see him sitting on the bed, but with the night sky clouded over there wasn't enough light to see his expression.

'You didn't do anything,' he said at length on a taut note. 'I was the one.'

'It takes two.' She tried to keep her own tone level. 'I could have said no.'

'You shouldn't have needed to.' He made a sudden impatient gesture. 'Anyway, that's water under the bridge. I've been making mistakes since the minute I clapped eyes on you, but I'll not be making any more. As soon as we get back to Sibu I'm putting you on a plane through to Singapore. You'll be home again in less than three days.'

Her throat had closed up. It took her all her time to force the words. 'That's all it meant to you—a mistake?'

'A self-indulgence might be closer the mark. I'm not making excuses for it because there aren't any. I just want you on that plane.' He slid between the sheets, turning on his side away from her.

Ria gazed unseeingly in the darkness. All over. Just like that. She felt numbed now but it wouldn't last. Nothing lasted.

'I think I hate you,' she said tonelessly, unable to stir herself to even that much emotion.

'Good.' He sounded totally unemotional himself. 'It's better that way. Get some sleep. We've an early start again in the morning.'

CHAPTER SEVEN

AUTUMN was a sad time, thought Ria, feeling the coolness in the air when she alighted from the bus. The trees along the suburban road were already beginning to lay a russet carpet; in another month they would be bare. Winter brought compensations, though. Steven loved the snow, Perhaps this year they might manage a week's break somewhere where the white stuff could be relied on to stay crisp and clean. Working for a travel agency had its advantages.

The terrace of pre-World War Two houses had a pleasing aspect in the early evening light, red brick façades subtly softened. Number eleven stood out from its immediate neighbours due to the riot of colour still pervading the small front garden. Ria used her latchkey to let herself into the house, picking up the envelope bearing her name from the hall table before tapping on the door immediately to her left. Another bill, no doubt. The only communications she ever received were bills and circulars. She was no great shakes at letter-writing herself, if it came to that, she reflected wryly, so why expect others to be? It wasn't as if she even knew anyone living far enough away that she didn't see them on a regular basis.

'Come in,' shouted a voice, muffled by the thickness of the panelled wood.

Ria turned the knob and went through into the large, square room with its comfortable furnishings and glowing gas fire.

'Turned cool, hasn't it?' greeted the grey-haired woman kneeling in front of the fire, raising the upper half of her body from its doubled-over position. 'Thought we'd got a leak, but it must have been me not lighting the burner quick enough. All right now, anyway.' She got to her feet, tucking her blouse back into the waistband of her skirt. 'He's out at the back with Clancy. You're early tonight.'

'I managed to make the five-thirty for once,' said Ria. 'No problems?'

Margaret Wright chuckled. 'Apart from being inundated with whys and wherefores since I fetched him home, not one. I never knew a four-year-old who could talk like that one. 'It's non-stop!' She tagged on swiftly, 'Not that I'm complaining. You know how I love having him.'

Ria smiled. 'Yes, I know. All the same, it will be a good thing all round when he starts school after Christmas, then he can exhaust his teacher instead. In the meantime, I've managed to get him into play-group four mornings a week instead of just two, starting next Monday.'

'Why not five?' suggested the older woman. 'Give you half a day to yourself at midweek at least.'

'I see little enough of him as it is,' Ria pointed out. 'Wednesday and Sunday are the only chances I get to spend any real time with him.'

'Well, if you and Keith want to get off on your own at all, you know where I am.'

'Thanks.' Ria knew she wouldn't be taking up that offer, but it didn't stop her being grateful for it. Without Margaret's help this past four years, she wouldn't have been able to take a job at all. With her own children all grown up and moved away, and her husband dead, it would have been understandable if she had preferred to enjoy her freedom, but she swore that looking after Steven kept her young. He called her Nana in lieu of any bona fide grandmother. Ria didn't mind. Margaret was closer than the aunt and uncle she so rarely saw these days.

He came running in now from the back garden, the tiny Yorkshire terrier at his heels. Tall for his age, and devoid of puppy fat, he was often taken for a couple of years older.

'I found a big mouse!' he shouted excitedly, holding out his cupped hands. 'I called him Snowy. Can I keep him, Mummy?'

'May I,' Ria corrected automatically before realising what she was implying. She added hastily, 'I don't think it's a very good idea, Steven. We don't have a cage. Anyway, if it's a tame one, it must belong to somebody already.'

'He wants to stay with me,' declared her son stubbornly. 'Look.'

A bewhiskered head poked out over his entwined fingers, pink nose twitching. Ria hid a smile. 'Point number one, it's a gerbil not a mouse,' she said. 'Point number two . . .'

'There's an old cage in the shed,' put in Margaret before she could complete the sentence. 'Used to be Rob's when he was a boy. Never got round to throwing it out. They don't take much looking after.'

Ria hesitated, seeing the conspiratorial glance that passed between woman and boy. Prearranged without a doubt. She supposed she should be cross, but it wasn't easy to haul Margaret over the coals considering all she did for them. They owed their home to her too.

'I can see I'm outnumbered,' she said resignedly. 'Only you'll have to be prepared to give him up if someone comes to ask about him, Steven.'

'I'll ask round,' declared the other woman comfortably. 'Just wait and I'll fetch the cage.'

Left alone with her son, Ria put out a hand and stroked the gerbil's head. If she had to give in she could at least do it with good grace. This was Margaret's house, after all. If she didn't mind, why complain? A boy needed pets. Clancy was getting too old to be classed as a playmate any more. He was asleep already in front of the fire.

'How was school today?' she asked softly, restraining herself from running her fingers through the thick dark hair. Steven hated being babied. If anything ever happened to him, she told herself now for the umpteenth time, she would die. He was her whole life.

'O.K., I think.' He was playing with the little animal, allowing it to run over his fingers, his small, well-defined features absorbed.

Ria sighed. 'You watch too much TV.'

'Television,' he corrected without looking up. 'You told me to say the proper name.'

Her laugh held a note of chagrin. 'I make nooses for my own neck! No,' she tagged on swiftly as his head lifted, 'it's just a silly saying.'

Margaret came back carrying the wire-fronted cage. 'I found a bag of sawdust too,' she announced, handing both items over. 'Feed it bread for tonight. I'll get it some proper food in the morning. Need any help upstairs?'

'I can manage, thanks.' Ria turned back to the door. 'See you tomorrow if not before.'

Steven ran ahead of her up the staircase, feet pounding the dark blue carpet. With the gerbil squirming in his hands he couldn't open the door. Ria had to put down both cage and food to do so. The room beyond was a replica in size and shape of the one below, furnished with a dining-table and chairs in addition to the comfortable three-piece suite. At the far end, and partitioned off from the rest by shelving, was the compact kitchenette. Further along the landing lay the main bedroom and tiny box-room where Steven slept, with the bathroom across from it. A self-contained flat such as this was worth a great deal more than was being charged, Ria knew, but Margaret had been more interested in finding the right occupants than in making a lot of money out of the conversion. It had been a lucky day when she had rung that bell for the first time.

With the gerbil safely housed and his future well mapped out, there was time for little else before Steven was rubbing his eyes and yawning. He insisted on having the cage on his bedside table, lying on his side to watch the animal explore its new domain.

'I'm going to buy him one of those wheels that go

round and round,' he murmured sleepily. 'I've got two pounds in my money box. Do you think that will be enough?'

'I should think so.' Ria could only hope no one would claim the gerbil. Another one just wouldn't be the same. She bent to kiss the smooth cheek, lingering for a moment to savour the fresh, sweet, after-bath smell of him. 'I love you,' she whispered.

'I love you, too,' came the mumbled reply. ' 'Night, Mummy.'

He was asleep before she had closed the door. Going back to the living-room, Ria glanced at her watch. Keith would be here in less than half an hour and she still had to peel the potatoes. He liked a hot meal in the evening, whereas she would have settled quite happily for a sandwich and an apple. Unfair, he always complained, when she never gained a pound no matter what she ate. He would be running to fat by the time he was in his mid-thirties if he wasn't careful. Already, at twenty-eight, he was showing distinct signs of an expanding waistline. Perhaps she should try putting him on a diet, she thought fondly. If carefully worked out, he needn't even know.

The meal still needed a quarter of an hour or so when he arrived. Ria met him at the door, lifting her mouth for his kiss. He looked weary, she thought, his pleasant, open features lacking in animation.

'They've upped my quota again,' he announced without preamble. 'Another hundred thousand on a year!'

'You shouldn't be so good at persuading people to sign on the dotted line,' she said with sympathy. 'Much always wants more. Anyway, you'll cope. You're the best they've got!'

'I'll try telling the area manager that next time I'm due for a salary review.' He was smiling now, cheered by the encouragement. 'Dinner ready yet? I'm famished!'

'Not quite. Why don't you sit down and have a drink while you're waiting?'

'Terrific idea.' He took the evening newspaper out of his jacket pocket before hanging the latter on the stand just inside the door. With tie and top button loosened, he gave vent to a sigh of relief. 'That's better. Now I can relax. Is there any lager?'

'In the fridge,' she said. 'I'll fetch it.'

He was watching television when she got back with the can and glass. Some kind of travel film, by the look of it. Ria poured the drink and set it ready on the small table at his elbow. The evening was following a familiar pattern. Not Keith's fault. She was the one who refused to leave Steven, and at this time of year there were few places they could take him. Keith never seemed to object. She supposed that after a long day selling insurance he was content to sit back and let go for a few hours.

It was high time she came to some definite decision regarding their future together, she acknowledged. He'd been so patient this past year. Steven needed a father, and he got on well enough with Keith. How many men were willing to take on a wife already burdened with another man's child? Not that she considered Steven a burden, of course, nor ever could. He was a vital part of her.

Standing behind the chair, she had been looking at the screen without really seeing the picture. Now, it suddenly sprang into focus as the commenator's voice impinged on her conscious mind. 'Tiny Sultanate of Brunei,' he was saying. 'Just opening up to tourism. Here in the capital of Bandar Seri Bagawan . . .'

Ria stopped listening again at that point, her mind turning inwards as she viewed once more the huge golden dome of the mosque, the Sultan's palace; Kampong Ayer with its stilted houses and teeming life. It was all coming back—all the things she had striven so hard to put behind her. Five years. A fifth of her total lifetime. She could see Ty's face as clearly as if it had been yesterday—but then, why not, considering she looked at his replica every day. A physical resemblance only, though. She would make sure Steven never acquired his father's disregard for other people's feelings.

The hurt was still there, deep though she had buried it, every freshly wakened memory a stab in the heart: the torment of that long journey home alone; the aching emptiness followed by weeks of utter despair when she realised she was pregnant. Her aunt and uncle had wanted her to have an abortion, but she had fought against it. Adoption had been one consideration until the moment they put the tiny, defenceless figure in her arms. Steven was all hers. She would have gone through fire and flood to keep him. As it turned out, it hadn't been necessary because Margaret had come to the rescue, but the feeling was the same.

'I think I can smell something burning,' said Keith, breaking in on her thoughts.

He was half-way out of the chair as he spoke. Ria put a restraining hand on his shoulder. 'Probably the potatoes boiling dry. I'll see to it.'

The saucepan was blackened on the bottom, but she managed to save most of the contents, mashing them with plenty of butter and milk to disguise any scorched taste. She felt churned up inside, her plans no longer cut and dried. Tonight she had been going to tell Keith she would marry him. Most of his evenings were spent round here as it was. He was a good man with a steady job (more echoes from the past). He would provide both her and Steven with a safe, secure future. A dullish one too, perhaps, yet that wasn't such a bad thing. She loved him as much as she was capable of loving any man these days.

Only it wasn't enough, was it? For the first time she forced herself to face facts. They had never slept together because she wouldn't allow him to stay the night while Steven slept in the next room. Only wouldn't it be more truthful to say it was because she hadn't wanted that kind of intimacy? Marriage wasn't going to alter basic emotion. If she felt no desire now she wasn't likely to feel it at all. Yet sex wasn't the be all and end all either, only a part of a relationship.

She was going around in circles and getting nowhere, she thought with resignation. The best thing to do was leave it until her mind was clearer—if that time ever came again. Right now it was a mess.

Keith left as usual around ten thirty. After taking a peep at Steven, Ria ran a warm bath, pinning up her hair against the steam. The face in the mirror formed a near perfect oval, the cheekbones prominent beneath eyes the colour of lapis lazuli. So different from five years ago, the way she was different. She had learned to hide her feelings instead of wearing them emblazoned on her sleeve, to conform with accepted standards of behaviour. These days she wore her hair long, painted her face with make-up, dressed in feminine clothes. She was still no great beauty, but men found her attractive—perhaps the more so because she remained aloof to their charms. There had been one other she had allowed into her life before Keith, only he had vanished after she told him about Steven.

Later, lying alone in the double bed, she tried to conjure sleep. Far from being relaxed by the bath, her body felt restless, tingling, her nerves tautly stretched.

She knew why, of course. The memories had come too sharp and clear to her mind. She could still remember the feel of Ty's hands, the touch of his lips, the hardness of his body. Such a gullible, unworldly little fool she had been then. Not that her worldliness went far beneath the surface now, if it came to that, only few would guess.

She slept at length, waking late and with little time to think about anything beyond getting Steven ready for play and herself ready for work. Today was Tuesday. Tomorrow there would be time and to spare for catching up on things. Given the choice, she would have preferred a whole weekend, but Saturday was their busiest time at the agency. One off in four was better than none at all, even if it was another three weeks to the next one.

It was belting down with rain, the wind moaning around the chimneypots. Wearing the military-style raincoat and matching trilby hat she had bought only the previous week, Ria felt at least well equipped for the weather. An umbrella would have been useless. The agency was situated in Regency Street, just one branch of an international company. First in, despite her rush, she got stuck straight into working out the quotation for a client's proposed tour of the Far East. It was complicated because he wanted to see everything in three weeks, but it was interesting. She wouldn't mind visiting Japan herself some day, she mused while checking air fares between Honshu and Hokkaido. Only it would have to wait until Steven was old enough to accompany her. She had already missed one promotion because of her unwillingness to take fact-finding trips abroad.

The morning passed swiftly. There was a run on; probably because of the weather, Ria thought. Nothing like the first breath of winter to make people start thinking about sun and sand. By eleven she was more than ready for the coffee break, although it had to be a case of a swallow when she could manage it between answering the myriad questions and calling up information on the computer.

'More like early May than October,' she commented wryly during a temporary lull to the man occupying the neighbouring hot seat. 'I'm shattered!'

'We haven't finished yet,' he said, eyeing the door which had just opened again. 'Here comes another one!'

Summoning a warm and welcoming smile, Ria turned to the front again, feeling the blood drain suddenly from her face as her eyes fell on the man who had just entered. He looked bigger than ever in the lightweight raincoat, was her first irrelevant thought. Thick and dark and sparkling with raindrops, his hair was tinged just faintly with grey now at the temples. Trust Ty not to bother touching it up. He was what he was, no pretence. In that respect, at least, he hadn't altered.

Hers was the closest position to the door, and therefore the one to which he directed his footsteps. 'I want to book a flight to Brunei with a stopover in Colombo,' he announced. 'Do you . . .' He broke off, a dawning incredulity in the grey eyes as he looked from her face down to the inset nameplate and back again. 'Ria?'

Her lips had gone dry. She put out the tip of her tongue to moisten them. 'Hallo, Ty,' she said huskily. 'This is a coincidence.'

'Isn't it?' He leaned an elbow on the high desk, regard interested, speculative, showing no hint of awkwardness. 'You look great! I'd hardly have known you if it weren't for those eyes. It's been years.'

'Yes.' She was uncomfortably conscious of the listening ears. Everyone here knew her circumstances and had met Steven. It wasn't going to take all that much intelligence to add two and two together if this conversation continued much further. She forced herself to smile, to shrug lightly. 'Anyway, nice to see you again. Now, about this flight . . .'

'It can wait. I'm still getting over the shock.' He slanted a glance in the direction of her fellow workers who were hardly bothering to conceal their curiosity, coming back to her face with a certain comprehension. 'How about lunch?'

'Swap with me, if you like,' offered Ria's neighbour before she could answer. 'I don't have anything planned.'

Ty nodded pleasantly to the younger man. 'Thanks.' One dark brow lifted as Ria continued to hesitate. 'For old times' sake?'

It was the last thing she wanted, Ria told herself, but she had to get him out of here before he gave too much away. She nodded, sliding from her chair. 'I'll get my coat.'

He was waiting by the door when she emerged from the rear. He watched her coming, eyes sliding the length of her down to her long, slender legs in their sheer dark hose and high-heeled black shoes. She was suddenly glad that she was wearing the new raincoat and hat. They afforded protection from far more than just the rain.

He took her to a small, unpretentious restaurant a couple of streets away—the only kind of place, Ria was bound to concede, where they were likely to get a table without a prior reservation at this hour. She left her wet outer things hanging alongside Ty's on the rack provided, trusting they would still be there when they were ready to leave. Ty was wearing a suit in a dark grey pinstripe. It wasn't a particularly good fit, Ria noted: the sleeves a fraction too short, the shoulders slightly narrow.

'Off the peg,' he said, catching her swift scrutiny and accurately guessing what was in her mind. 'I didn't have time to get one made up before the funeral.'

Her eyes sought his. 'Funeral?'

'My father. Last week. I got there with twenty-four hours to spare.'

'I'm sorry.' She scarcely knew what else to say. 'You weren't very close, were you?'

He gave her a thoughtful glance. 'How did you know that?'

Ria could have kicked herself. Did she want him to think she had spent the last five years keeping her memory of him alive? 'Something Jack once told me,' she said evasively. 'How is he, by the way?'

A muscle jerked suddenly in the strong jawline. 'Jack died two years ago.'

'Oh.' She felt choked, suddenly on the verge of tears. She made a supreme effort to gain control of herself. 'How did it happen?'

'He fell overboard one night. We never found his body.' The tone was measured. 'Sorry to spring it on you. There was no other way.'

'That's all right.' She kept her own voice steady. 'It was all a long time ago. So what are you doing with yourself now?'

Broad shoulders lifted in a shrug. 'Much the same. I was in Belaga a couple of months back. Jemo used the money you left to move down there so that Tamo could have a proper home while he was schooling. She married Rahim six months later. They say they have us to thank for bringing them together. Seems Rahim took her under his wing as soon as he realised who she was.'

'Really?' Ria was genuinely delighted. 'Oh, that's wonderful!'

'She said she never heard from you again,' he continued levelly. 'Would an occasional letter have gone amiss?'

Ria bit her lip. How to get round the fact that she had wanted no reminders of the time she had spent in Borneo. 'You yourself told me it was best to forget it,' she said. 'When I thought it through, it seemed the best way.'

He accepted the statement without comment. 'So tell me your news,' he invited instead. 'You're still a Miss according to your nameplate.'

'Not for much longer,' she claimed without pause for consideration. 'I'm getting married at the end of the year.'

His face dropped fleetingly to her left hand toying with her fork. 'He doesn't believe in long engagements?'

'I don't wear my ring at work' she prevaricated swiftly. 'It's too easy to lose.' She laughed. 'Keith's in insurance. It makes me conscious of the risks.'

'Better to be safe than sorry,' he quipped, sounding faintly sardonic. 'You've certainly altered your viewpoint!'

'I was just a kid,' she returned, fighting down the urge to say something scathing in reply. 'I've grown up since then.'

'More than a little,' he agreed. 'You filled out in all the right places, that's for sure!'

The pale blue uniform blouse she was wearing, Ria knew, emphasised her figure. She refused to allow her own eyes any downward cast. 'I was speaking about emotions,' she said. 'If there's one favour you did me, Ty, it was in making me realise that the vast majority of men are only out for what they can get!'

There was no reaction that she could see in the lean features. 'But not your fiancé?'

'No, not Keith. He's one of the few exceptions.'

'Good for him. Maybe you should introduce us.'

'I don't think so. You'd have nothing in common.'

'Or maybe he doesn't know about your past,' he mocked, ignoring the last.

'Of course he knows!' Ria was goaded beyond discretion for a moment. 'I could hardly have kept it a secret when ...' She broke off abruptly, catching her breath at the thought of what she had almost let slip. Ty mustn't know—mustn't even suspect. How had they managed to get to this point in so short a time?

The grey eyes had narrowed a fraction, intent on her face. 'You were saying?' he prompted.

'There should be no secrets between man and wife,' she substituted lamely.

'So you've told him about every man you ever knew?'

'There haven't ...' She stopped again, biting her lip, this time making no attempt to amend the slip.

'Haven't been any others,' he finished for her on a satirical note, and drew a chilly blue glance.

'Is that so difficult to believe?'

'The way you were, yes.' His tone had deepened reminiscently. 'I've never forgotten you, Ria.'

Her laugh sounded harsh. 'So much so it took you whole minutes to recognise me just now!'

'I was hardly expecting to see you,' he defended himself. 'Especially not looking the way you do. In my mind's eye you were still the little bit of a thing in jeans and T-shirt I last saw at the airport in Sibu that morning. There's no trace of her now!'

More than he knew, she thought bitterly. He still had the same effect on her: still made her pulses race, her nerves tingle. That programme last night had been a warning that he was coming back into her life. Only it wasn't going to be for long.

'It's been five years,' she said, forcing herself to meet the grey eyes. 'Nothing stands still. You don't intend staying in England now your father's gone, then?'

He shook his head. 'There's nothing to stay for. I was cut out of the will years back.'

'There's your mother and sister.'

'Teresa's married, with a family of her own. My mother . . .' he paused, shrugging, 'she's nothing if not self-sufficient. They don't need me, any more than I need them.' There was brief silence while he studied her, an odd look in his eyes. 'What else did Jack tell you about me?'

'Nothing,' she said. 'That was the sum and total of what he knew at the time. I don't expect you ever got round to confiding more.'

'I'm not sure. I don't even remember telling him that much, so who knows?' He took the bottle from the basket and poured more wine for them both. 'What time do you have to be back at work?'

'In about twenty minutes.'

'Doesn't give us much time.'

Her head lifted sharply. 'For what?'

'To talk over old times.' He was smiling a little. 'I don't suppose you could have dinner with me tonight?'

'You're right, I couldn't,' she said, smothering her involuntary response to the question.

'Fiancé wouldn't like it?'

'That's one reason.' She didn't bother to itemise others. 'If you still want us to handle the flight reservations for you it will take a couple of days to get the tickets through.'

'That's all right. I didn't plan on leaving before the twenty-third.'

That was only a week away. She said softly, 'Back to the *Tiger Rose*?'

'I don't have the *Tiger Rose* any more. I moved on to something a bit bigger.' He caught her reaction, mouth twisting. 'Like you said, it's been five years. A lot can happen.'

'Yes.' She felt unaccountably depressed. Without thinking about it, she tagged on, 'What's in Colombo?'

'A friend.' He said it without expression. 'I'll need at least three days, by the way.'

'Fine. That shouldn't present any difficulties.' Ria stirred restlessly, glancing again at her watch. 'I think I should be getting back.'

'We haven't had coffee yet.'

'I know.' She made an apologetic gesture. 'All the same . . .'

'I'll get the bill,' he said, lifting a hand to attract their waiter's attention. 'Can't have you late back.'

It had stopped raining when they got outside, although the skies remained dark and overcast. A chilly wind was rapidly drying off the wet pavements. Ria shivered and pulled up the collar of her coat.

'You must hate this,' she commented. 'At least where you came from it's warm in the rain!'

'I couldn't stick it here for long,' he agreed. 'Come on, I'll walk you back.'

'There's no need.'

'I know, but I'll need to pay for the tickets in advance, I imagine.' He took hold of her arm, drawing her out of the path of a man forging along with head bent against the wind. 'The shipping lanes are dangerous places to be if you're not paying attention.'

Ria was vibrantly aware of the feel of his fingers under her elbow; they seemed to burn right through her clothing to her skin. He was close enough to dwarf her with his size, close enough to leave the faint, elusive smell of aftershave lingering in her nostrils. The man she had known had never bothered to use such refinements. When in Rome? she thought. He was still so much of an enigma.

It took bare minutes to walk back to the agency. They spoke little on the way. With the moment of leavetaking on her, Ria could find few words. It was left to Ty to take the initiative, seizing her by the shoulders and drawing her firmly to him.

'For old times' sake,' he said, and kissed her on the lips.

Taken totally by surprise, Ria had no opportunity to gather herself against the onslaught of sensation. It was as if the years had been stripped away. For a fleeting instant she found herself returning the kiss, mouth blindly seeking, and then, as realisation dawned, tearing herself away with a choked little exclamation.

She left him standing there on the pavement amid the amused smiles of passers-by, heading indoors as if all the devils in hell were hot on her heels.

CHAPTER EIGHT

TY made no attempt to follow her. It was a moment or two before she remembered he was supposed to come in and complete the financial side of the transaction. Her response had done it, she concluded unhappily. For a moment there he had got through her guard—and recognised the fact. There were other agencies. Perhaps he deemed it wiser to leave well alone. He should have thought of that before he kissed her—except that he couldn't have been expected to anticipate such a strong reaction. It had taken her by surprise too. She simply hadn't realised just how deeply he had got to her.

'You look bewitched, bothered and not a little bewildered,' commented the man who had exchanged his lunch hour with her, coming to his feet as she passed the desk. 'Not run into any trouble, I hope?'

Ria gave him a brief, unseeing glance, summoning a vague smile. 'It's cold out. Sorry if I held you up.'

'You're not due back for another five minutes,' he called after her. 'Take your time.'

The small cloakroom was mercifully empty. Ria hung up her coat and hat and tidied her hair before the wash-basin mirror. Her eyes looked huge and dark, her face unnaturally flushed. Five years, and it could have been yesterday. What price peace of mind now?

It wasn't going to make any difference, though, was it? she thought bitterly. Ty might have been intrigued enough by the apparent changes in her to try an impulsive experiment, but he had been quick to depart once the message went home. He wouldn't be back, that was for sure. He'd had trouble enough getting rid of her last time without risking a repetition.

Her cheeks burned afresh at the memory of that final night before her departure from Sibu. She had gone to his berth out in the saloon and pleaded with him to let her stay—sinking every last vestige of pride in her desperation to be with him. Only he hadn't cared. He'd told her roughly to get back to her cabin and stop making a fool of herself. Next time he needed a woman, he had said, he would make sure it was one and not some silly little girl with romantic notions. Callous and cruel, that was Ty. On the face of it, he hadn't changed one iota.

The door behind her opened suddenly to admit one of the other young women she worked with.

'Are you all right?' asked the other. 'Colin thought you looked upset.'

Ria pulled herself together. 'I'm fine,' she acknowledged. 'Just windswept. I'll be out in a minute, Pat.'

'There's no hurry.' Pat hesitated, her small pointed face avid with a curiosity barely held in check. 'Tell me to mind my own business, if you like, but that man you went off with *is* Steven's father, isn't he?'

Ria eyed her levelly. 'What makes you think that?'

'Because he looks so much like him. Steven, I mean. Was it really pure chance that he just happened to walk in here?'

'So he tells me. I've no reason to disbelieve him.'

'Isn't that just fantastic? He isn't a bit as I'd imagined him. I mean, when you told us about Steven, you only said . . .'

'When I told you about Steven it was because I knew you'd seen me with him that day in town and I wanted to stop any speculation around the office before it got started.' Ria's tone was wry. 'Seems I didn't succeed.'

'We're only human. Of course we've wondered who his father was.' Pat was only semi-apologetic. 'He's quite a bit older than you, isn't he?'

'He was thirty-two when it happened,' Ria said shortly, 'and I was twenty. We were in Borneo at the time. That should give all of you plenty to get your teeth into! Now, if you don't mind, I've got work to do.'

She pushed past before the other could say anything else, marching back into the office looking neither to left or right. Colin hadn't yet gone. Ria said coolly, 'In future, if you want to know anything, ask me yourself.'

He flushed. 'I was worried about you. You went through here as if you'd seen a ghost. Sorry if Pat got inquisitive. I should have known better than to ask her to see if you were O.K.'

The anger drained from her suddenly, leaving her flat and empty. 'I'm the one who should know better,' she said ruefully. 'Sorry, Colin.'

'Think nothing of it. Pat can be a real pain in the neck at times.' He gave her a cheery smile. 'Anyway, I'm off. I promised June I'd pick up her watch from the jewellers. She's been having it cleaned. See you later.'

There had never been an afternoon so long. Ria spent most of it catching up on paperwork. By twenty past five she was more than ready for home. Pat was offhand in saying good night, obviously still smarting from the put-down she had received earlier. Ria couldn't find it in herself to regret the moment. Curiosity could be taken too far.

She took the tube to East Finchley, then the bus. By twenty minutes past six she was putting her key in the door. For thirty-six glorious hours she was her own boss. Keith was out of town until Thursday, which meant she and Steven had all the time in the world to be together. Tomorrow she planned on taking him to the Planetarium; he was old enough now to appreciate the spectacle.

He was ready and waiting, the gerbil cage securely held. 'Snowy and me had chocolate cake for tea,' he announced the moment Ria entered the room.

'Not to mention the sausage and chips!' chuckled Margaret behind him.

The combination made Ria wince, but she said nothing. Margaret had brought up three children of her own on the same kind of food without apparent harm to any of them. It was difficult to tell her she had been totally wrong. On one occasion, Ria had suggested letting Steven wait until she got home herself to have a meal, but the other had been upset at the idea of the 'poor little mite' going so long. It wasn't good for him to go to bed on a full stomach, anyway, she had declared, clinching the argument.

'I'm going round to babysit for Lucy tonight,' she added now, 'so you'll have the house to yourself. Don't forget to put the bolt on the front door before you go to bed, will you? I shan't be back till about lunchtime.'

'I'll remember,' Ria promised. 'Enjoy yourself.'

'I will, that. It isn't often I get the chance to spoil that granddaughter of mine.'

Ria laughed. 'Yes, well, don't overdo it or you might not get the chance again!'

She was still smiling as she drew Steven out into the hall and closed the door. Margaret was incorrigible! The sudden ring of the front-door bell startled her for a moment.

'I'll get it,' she called back into the room. 'Steven, you're going to drop that cage if you're not careful! Hold it in both hands.'

She was opening the door as she spoke, head half turned to look back at her son. Looking in front of her again she felt the smile freeze on her lips, just the way it had done earlier that day. For several seconds she just stood gazing at the man standing on the step, unable to make her mind function.

Ty was the first to break the silence. 'I was going to go away and come back again later,' he said, 'but then I thought why not strike right away.' He was smiling. 'Are you going to invite me in?'

'How did you know?' Ria's voice sounded faint and faraway.

'Quite simple. I followed you when you left the office.'

'Why?'

He shrugged. 'Call it a sudden whim. I intended meeting you as you left work, but I had this notion you might just decide to turn awkward. Anyway, here I am.'

'Which still doesn't answer the question,' she said, mind slowly wakening to the full implications of the situation. *'Why,* Ty?'

The grey eyes studied her, expression difficult to assess. 'I thought we needed to talk.'

'Who is it, Mummy?' Steven poked his head between Ria's hip and the door, looking up inquisitively at the visitor. 'Hallo? I'm Steven. What's your name?'

In the following pause, Ria could almost taste the tension. She stood there woodenly, seeing the dawning realisation in Ty's eyes with a sickening, sinking feeling in her stomach. He knew. There was no way he couldn't know. The resemblance between man and child was uncanny. As if registering the atmosphere, Steven himself made no attempt to repeat the question, sticking a thumb in his mouth as he sometimes still did when perplexed.

Once again it was Ty who spoke first. 'I think you'd definitely better let me in,' he said tautly.

Short of shutting the door in his face, there was nothing Ria could do but comply.

'We're upstairs,' she told him. 'Take the cage up, Steven, before you spill all the sawdust out of it.'

The child went on ahead. Ty watched him go, mouth a thin, straight line. 'Why didn't you let me know?' he demanded.

'Why assume he's yours?' she clipped back. 'Or do you imagine I was pining so much for you I couldn't even think of being with any other man?'

The look he gave her was heavy with irony. 'Don't insult my intelligence. I was glancing through some family albums only the other day. He could be me at that age.' He moved restlessly. 'Anyway, we can't talk about it down here.'

'We can hardly discuss it in front of Steven either,' she pointed out.

'All right then, so we'll wait until you've put him to bed. I don't have anything else planned for the evening.'

'And you're naturally taking it for granted I'm free too.'

'If you're not, you'd better arrange it.'

Ria shrugged, assuming a nonchalance she was far from feeling. 'As a matter of fact, Keith is out of town for a couple of days, so the question is academic. Be my guest.'

'Does he live here with you?' demanded Ty, following her up the stairs.

'No, he doesn't!' The reaction was too strong; she made some attempt to temper it. 'He isn't the kind of man to expect the comforts without the commitment.'

'Bully for him,' on a caustic note. 'Some of us are just too good for this life!'

Steven came running from the direction of his bedroom as they reached the landing. He had got over his momentary shyness now, his face alight with interest. Guests other than Keith were rare. Whoever this man was, he promised a break in the familiar routine—perhaps even a delaying of the dreaded bedtime.

'You never said your name,' he accused. 'I told you mine.'

'This is Mr Morgan,' said Ria before Ty could answer. 'Be a gentleman, Steven, and open the door.'

There was a faint snort from behind, but no other comment. Ty followed her into the room, sweeping a cursory glance over the furnishings.

'This place must be costing you a packet,' he stated flatly. 'Does your job pay that well?'

'Well enough for what Margaret charges me, and considering the allowances I get as a single parent.' Ria was determined not to let him anger her in any way. 'That's the lady who owns the house. I was lucky to find her.'

'Very.' From his tone it was obvious that he was not convinced. 'I could use a drink,' he added. 'That's whisky you've got on the sideboard over there, isn't it?'

'Keith likes a whisky and soda after a meal,' she

returned with deliberation. 'The only reason I keep it in. Help yourself.'

He poured a generous measure, tossing half of it back at a single swallow before turning with the glass in his hand to look across the room at her and smile thinly. 'I needed that!'

'Hot tea is supposed to be a better remedy for shock,' she suggested on a dry note. 'I'll make us both some, shall I? I'm afraid I can't offer you dinner. I didn't bother getting anything in.'

'I'm not hungry right now,' he said. 'You've knocked the stuffing right out of me.'

Steven had been listening to the conversation with mounting impatience. Grown-ups did so much talking together! He went to fetch one of his books, tugging at the visitor's sleeve.

'If you're staying, will you read to me?'

Ty looked down at the diminutive figure of his son, expression undergoing a subtle alteration. When he smiled it softened his whole face. 'Just let me get my coat off first and we'll see about it,' he promised. The glance he shot at Ria was a challenge in itself. 'While your mother makes the tea.'

It took her more than a few minutes because she made some sandwiches too. It was going to be a lengthy session, and it was a long time since lunch. It seemed an age since the morning when none of this had happened. If only Ty had chosen some other travel agency to handle his arrangements. The twenty-third, he had said. One short week in which to come to terms with his new status. Tonight wasn't going to be the last of it, for certain. Whatever his faults, he would probably want to make some financial reparation. For Steven's sake, she would take it, too. Pride at all costs was a pure self-indulgence. Jemo had taught her that much a long, long time ago.

They were sitting together on the sofa when she took the tray through, dark heads bent to the book in Ty's hands. He had taken off both coat and jacket, his tie loosened the same way Keith liked to loosen his. In the plain white shirt, with both sleeves rolled, he looked much more the man she had known. Ria felt as if an iron hand had gripped her heart.

'And that,' he said, finishing the story, 'was that.'

'Another,' Steven begged, obviously enjoying the experience. His fingers turned the pages eagerly, searching for a tried and true favourite. 'This one!'

'Not right now,' said his father easily. 'I'll tell you what, though, we'll do that one when you're in bed.'

Steven looked crestfallen for a moment but soon recovered. Sulking was outside his experience. 'O.K.,' he responded.

Ty laughed and ruffled his hair. 'Go and play with something while your mother and I have some tea.'

Accepting the cup Ria had poured for him, he added softly, 'You've done a good job. He's a terrific kid!'

'Thanks.' She couldn't deny the glow of warmth the approbation brought her. 'I've had help.'

The strong features darkened again. 'From this Keith?'

'No, from Margaret downstairs. She looks after him for me while I'm at work. Fetches him from school and all that.'

'He's at school already?'

'Not proper school—playgroup.'

Grey eyes studied her for a moment, narrowed reflectively. 'Why didn't you get in touch once you found out you were pregnant?'

Ria shrugged. 'You'd made it pretty clear I was nothing more than an encumbrance to you. What difference would it have made?'

'One hell of a lot.' Ty sounded suddenly savage. 'Do you think I'd have left you to go through all this on your own?'

'Do you think I'd have wanted you coming after me just because you felt you had to?' she demanded with equal ferocity. She was sitting on the extreme edge of her seat, eyes dark with the anger she had sworn to forgo. 'It was my responsibility, not yours.'

'You're saying I don't have any rights?'

Ria stared at him, pulses jumping all over the place. 'If you ever had you certainly don't now,' she got out. 'He's mine, Ty!'

They had been speaking in low voices despite the atmosphere between them. Steven was delving in his toy box at the far end of the room, oblivious to everything else. Ria made a valiant effort to regain control of the situation.

'If you hadn't wandered into the agency this morning you'd never have known about him. Isn't it easier after all this time to just leave things the way they are? If you wanted to settle something on him for the future I wouldn't say no.'

'Thanks.' The sarcasm bit. 'Money covers everything, is that what you're saying?'

'If you can't afford it . . .' she began, and left it right there as his teeth came together with an audible snap.

'You've changed in more ways than just one,' he clipped. 'The girl I knew would have shown more finesse!'

'The girl you knew was a silly little romantic with her head in the clouds,' she hissed back at him, lowering her voice again as Steven glanced their way. 'I learned to hit back.'

'You certainly did.' Ty put down the half-empty cup, taking advantage of the pause to gather himself. When he spoke again it was in modulated, reasonable tones. 'Ria, it wasn't the way you thought back then. I no more wanted to lose you than you wanted to go, only it wouldn't have worked out. You needed a home, boy-friends, parties—all the things you'd missed out on trying to be what you weren't. All I could offer you was a rusting boat and a life where even I couldn't be sure what the next day was going to bring.'

'I see.' She attempted the same level delivery. 'So you sent me away for my own sake. Self-sacrificing of you, Ty—if I believed a word of it!'

'It's true enough,' he returned doggedly. 'Believe it or

not. You were the best thing that ever happened to me. There were even moments when I saw myself turning over a whole new chapter.'

Ria was silent for several moments, her throat aching with a new kind of pain. 'But you got over it.'

'Yes, I got over it. Or I thought I had.' He paused, watching her. 'Seeing you again behind that counter this morning was like being socked on the jaw. I couldn't leave it at that.'

'Don't.' She was trembling, trying not to let herself read too much into what he was saying. 'You're only going to be here another week, Ty. Why didn't you just let it go?'

His smile lacked humour. 'You think this doesn't change my plans? For God's sake, Ria, I've just found out I've got a four-year-old son! You really expect me to just walk away?'

'You'll do it eventually, so why not now?' It was difficult to force the words out. 'I neither want nor need anything from you.'

'But you're not immune either,' he said softly. 'Any more than I am. When I kissed you a few hours ago we went back the whole five years. Why else do you think I had to follow you here?'

'If it was in the hope of a quick tumble in bed for old times' sake, you'd have been disappointed anyway,' she retorted, and saw his mouth tilt.

'I suppose I left myself wide open for that one.'

'You could say so.' She got abruptly to her feet, raising her voice to call to the boy still playing across the room. 'Come on, Steven, it's time for your bath.'

He obeyed without a murmur of protest, much to her relief, pausing in front of Ty to say anxiously, 'You won't forget what you promised, will you?'

'I won't forget.' The smile was genuine this time. 'As soon as you're tucked in I'll be there.'

Ria ran the bath while Steven undressed himself. He had been independent from a very early age. It took her all her time to stop herself from hugging the wiry little body to her as he climbed into the warm water. He quite liked hugging at bedtime, and on special occasions, but not when there was serious business afoot. The bath was for boat-sailing once the washing was out of the way: ten minutes ploughing the high seas. More shades of his father, came the unwilling thought now. He had never been on a real boat. Perhaps she had subconsciously avoided the experience.

Refusing to leave a four-year-old alone in a bath, Ria always joined in the game. Steven usually put her in charge of the enemy craft, chasing and sinking the latter with great splashings and noisy sound effects. Margaret had said jokingly on more than one occasion that it sounded as if they might both be coming through the ceiling any minute.

Tonight was no exception to the rule. It stunned her all the more when he said out of the blue, 'Mummy, why were you and Mr Morgan quarrelling?'

'We weren't,' she denied, breaking a golden rule not to lie to the boy. There were times when all rules had to be bent a little. She was angry both with herself and with Ty for not waiting to say what had to be said after Steven had gone to bed. Little pitchers had big ears. He hadn't appeared to be taking any notice, but the atmosphere had obviously affected him. 'It was a just a discussion,' she added lamely. 'Grown-ups sometimes get a bit carried away when they're talking.'

The words themselves might have been over his head, but the explanation seemed to suffice. For a moment or two he played quite happily before pulling her up short again by saying calmly, 'Why don't I have a daddy like other boys?'

Ria swallowed hard on the lump in her throat. It was the first time he had actually voiced the question, although she had been anticipating it for some time. She had had an answer all prepared, but it scarcely fitted the bill now. Ty was there in the other room. How could she tell his son she didn't know where he was? Yet she had to say something.

'I'm thinking of getting you one,' she managed with creditable steadiness. 'You like Uncle Keith, don't you?'

He considered the question in all seriousness, head tilted to one side. 'I'd rather have Mr Morgan,' he pronounced at length with childish candour. 'Uncle Keith doesn't read to me like he does.'

That was true enough, Ria was bound to acknowledge. The hardness in her throat was threatening to choke her. Keith lacked any real understanding where children were concerned, although he tried hard enough to find the right wavelength. Ty hadn't talked down to the child, nor had he attempted to curry favour by indulging his desire for more of the same. At least not on the spot. Children respected a firm answer. They knew where they were.

None of which was of any real help at this moment. A compromise was the only possible way out.

'Mr Morgan isn't going to be here very long,' she said. 'So I'm afraid we don't have any choice. Time to get dry if you're going to have that story he promised you.'

Ty came through to the little bedroom as soon as she called. Lit by the soft glow of the lamp, the smallness became cosiness, the soft yellow walls and carpet a background for the practical white melamine furnishings loaded with books and stuffed animals.

'Hi, feller,' he said to the gerbil in its cage by the bedside, sticking in a finger for the little creature to sniff as he sat down on the bed. 'Just don't take the end off, that's all!'

'Snowy doesn't bite people he likes,' Steven assured him.

'Looks as if I've found favour, then.' Ty had brought the book from which he had been reading earlier through with him. He settled himself more comfortably against the headrest. 'Right, let's get started. Page fourteen, wasn't it?'

'Sixteen,' Steven corrected. 'It's about space.'

'A bit advanced for me, but I'll do my best.' Grey

eyes lifted in Ria's direction. 'Do we let your mother stay?'

Steven chuckled. 'Yes.'

'For which great favour I am truly grateful,' said Ria drily, 'but I happen to have some washing up to do.'

'It's done.' There was a sardonic edge to Ty's smile. 'No sweat. It isn't the first time I washed up a few dishes. Why don't you sit down and listen? You might learn something.'

Ria sat, too bemused to do anything else. Listening to the deep, masculine voice over those following few minutes, she was transported across the miles and the years to a magical afternoon by a jungle river. Wrapped in each other's arms, they had talked about so many things. When she closed her eyes she could almost smell the damp heat, hear the shrill buzzing of cicadas, the rustling of the undergrowth as a million and one tiny unseen creatures went about their daily business. She had loved this man then. He had meant everything to her. If she was to believe what he said now, he had felt more for her than he had eventually made out, but it hadn't been enough. It still wouldn't be.

She came back to the present as the story ended, pleased when Steven made no attempt to press for more.

'Thank you for reading it to me,' he said, snuggling down between the sheets. The face looking up at the man now standing was wistful. 'Mummy says you could be my daddy if you weren't going away again,' he stated. 'Do you have to go?'

'No,' came the soft reply. 'And I'd be proud to be your daddy.'

'That's all right, then.' The blue-grey eyes closed, lashes curling downy soft over pink cheeks. 'G'night.'

CHAPTER NINE

Ria avoided Ty's eyes as she went to kiss her son good night. He was standing at the door when she straightened again, leaving her with no alternative but to join him.

'He misunderstood,' she said quietly, still not meeting his gaze. 'I didn't say anything of the kind.'

Ty drew her outside and closed the door before answering, mouth twisted, 'That I can imagine. All the same, he's my son.'

'Biologically speaking, perhaps, not otherwise. The formative years are the most important when it comes to developing relationships.'

'Maybe. It hasn't stopped him from missing a father figure, has it? Obviously your Keith is no substitute.'

Ria swallowed painfully. 'Leave Keith out of it. You don't know anything about him!'

'I'm going to, though, because you're going to tell me.'

She said furiously, 'You can't walk in here after five years making demands, Ty!'

'Oh yes, I can.' The hand still holding her arm firmed its grip. 'Let's go back to the living-room before we wake him up again.'

He was right, she was bound to concede. This was hardly the place to conduct an argument. Margaret had already left the house; she had heard the front door close half an hour ago. It was just the two of them now.

She sank into one of the armchairs when they reached the room, aware of the trembling in her lower limbs. Reaction to all this, she thought wryly. Was it any wonder? Ty sat down on the sofa opposite, gaze uncompromising.

'All right,' he said, 'so let's have the truth. Are you engaged to this man or aren't you?'

Her chin remained high. 'He wants me to marry him.'

'But you haven't given him an answer yet?'

'Not in so many words.'

'Stop prevaricating,' he growled. 'Yes or no?'

'All right then, no.' She added quickly, 'That doesn't mean I don't intend saying yes.'

'If you're that unsure, he isn't the right man for you.' The statement was unequivocal. 'How did you meet him, anyway?'

'He came to do a life policy for me. I had to have some protection for Steven's future in case anything happened to me.'

'Commendable. How long ago was that?'

'About fourteen months.'

'And he's had his feet under the table ever since.' He was leaning back in the cushions, hands clasped behind his head, one leg slung across the other knee. The tie had gone, Ria noted, his shirt unbuttoned at the neck. He looked like a man settled for the evening in his own home. 'Why did you make out you had the wedding all fixed?' he asked now, jerking her back to the topic in hand.

'Self-defence,' she said without thinking, then did a hasty reshuffle as his brows lifted. 'Pride, vanity, call it what you like. I suppose I didn't want you to think I'd spent the last five years eating my heart out for you.'

'It can't have been easy.' There was no trace of irony in his voice. 'I don't imagine there are all that many men willing to take on somebody else's kid.'

'Would you?'

'Irrelevant. He *is* my kid.' The pause held deliberation. 'Question is, what we're going to do about it?'

'It's simple enough,' she said. 'You get up and walk out of here and forget you saw either of us. That way we'll all be happier.'

'Like hell.' He was angry but holding it in check. 'I don't leave here till we've got things sorted out.'

She said huskily, 'And how do you propose doing it?'

It was a moment before he moved, eyes reflective as he looked at her. When he straightened it was with purpose. 'We can start with ourselves,' he said, getting to his feet.

Ria shrank back as far as she could in the chair as he came towards her, putting up both hands in panicky rejection. 'No, Ty! It's no answer!'

'It's a beginning.' He pulled her upright, holding her there in front of him with his hands curving her face, mouth unrelenting. 'We've a lot of catching up to do, Ria. Five whole years of it.'

She was stiff when he kissed her, but it didn't last. The feel of him, the scent of him, the heat surging through her, they were all too much to withstand. She went on her toes to reach him, sliding both arms about his neck and kissing him back with a kind of desperation. He was so solid, so real. No matter what the underlying emotion, his desire was as urgent as hers. Her body moved involuntarily against him, seeking closer contact, remembering. She couldn't get close enough. Not this way with all the encumbering clothing between them. She wanted to be back on that river bank, naked and unashamed, indifferent even to the things that crawled and flew in the sultry afternoon heat. Her lips murmured his name, softly, pleadingly.

Only when Ty swung her up in his arms did sense return for a moment. She began to struggle, to protest, but he held her firm.

'Don't fight me,' he said. 'You want this as much as I do.'

'It hasn't even been twelve hours,' she whispered.

He shook his head. 'Twelve hours or twelve years, it wouldn't make any difference. I'm taking you to bed, Ria. The one place we can get back to where we were. Just accept it.'

Her bedroom was dark and cool. Setting her on her feet again, Ty switched on both lamps, looking at the double bed with a faint twist of his lips.

'I want to see you,' he said when she made a sound of dissent. 'All of you.'

He came back to where she stood, taking her in his arms again to kiss her into quivering acquiescence, long lean fingers sliding the buttons of her blouse. Her breasts filled his palms when he cupped them from beneath. He bent his head to kiss each tender, swollen nipple, fingers unfastening the clip on her waistband to push the blue skirt down over her hips. She was wearing little under it. Ria caught her breath at the sheer sensation of his hands on her skin, muscle and sinew tensed to his touch. But only for a moment, then she was pliable again, responding, emotions soaring to carry her far beyond any lingering reservations. They were together, and nothing had changed.

Ty lifted her on to the bed before taking off his own clothing. Ria watched dreamily, drinking in the tanned muscularity. Five years had made little physical difference. He looked just as hard, just as fit—just as devastatingly male. She reached for him hungrily when he came to her, the need overflowing. She had never stopped loving him; she knew that now. The memory of him had coloured her life. Whatever happened afterwards, she had to have tonight.

He took her slowly, even tenderly, making it last until they could neither of them bear another moment. Ever-decreasing circles, thought Ria mistily as the frenzy of that final, surging release fell away. For the first time in years she was whole again.

She awoke to her inner alarm at seven, her recall instant and total.

Ty was still asleep, face buried in the pillows, dark hair roughened. One arm lay heavy across her waist, his bare thigh so close she could feel the hair on it tickling her skin. It was warm beneath the duvet—and safe. While she lay still he would stay asleep, and the future with him. She didn't want to think beyond this moment. There were too many sharp corners waiting.

In spite of her stillness, he stirred, head turning her way. His eyes were open, expression fully aware.

'Good morning,' he said softly.

Ria steeled herself as his hand began a questing exploration, catching and holding it before it could discover too much. There were things they had to talk about—matters which last night had glossed over. Steven was her first concern, now and always. She wasn't going to forget that again.

'I'll make us some coffee,' she said, pushing his arm away.

'What time do you have to be at work?' he asked, refusing to let her go.

'I don't,' she was bound to admit. 'It's my day off.'

'In that case, the coffee can wait.'

'No!' This time she succeeded in breaking free, half-way to getting out of the bed until she realised she would have to walk naked across the room to reach her house-coat draped over the chair. It was ridiculous, she knew, after the night they had just spent, but she couldn't make herself do it. Not right at this minute, at any rate.

'That's better,' said Ty as she sank back into the pillows again. He came up on an elbow above her, studying her face with a quizzical expression in his eyes. 'What are you afraid of?'

Myself, she could have told him. What I feel about you; what I'm pretty sure you don't feel about me. She shook her head dumbly, unable to find any reasonable alternative to the truth. Let him sort it out for himself. He was bright enough. 'It's too late for regrets,' he stated when she failed to reply. There was a faint edge to his voice. 'It was too late the moment you opened that door to me last night.'

'It isn't too late to feel ashamed of myself for letting it happen like that,' she forced out through stiff lips, and saw his mouth tilt.

'You didn't let it; I didn't give you any option. One thing we proved, it's all still there. That has to make things easier.'

Her brow creased. 'What things?'

'Making a go of it. We're going to make that son of ours legitimate.'

'You mean marriage?'

'I don't know of a better way. Do you?'

'You could give him your name by deed poll, if it's that important,' Ria said, trying to retain some measure of control. 'There's no stigma attached these days anyway.'

'Tell that to the marines! No kid of mine is going through life with a label round his neck.'

Ria turned her face away. 'You didn't even know you had one up to yesterday.'

'So I made a fast adjustment.' Ty put a hand beneath her chin, forcing her to look at him. 'It's my right to have a hand in his upbringing. If I'd known about him from the start and left the two of you to fend for yourselves, that would be another matter. Maybe I should have guessed what might happen, considering I never took any precautions, but I swear it never once crossed my mind.'

'I suppose,' she said woodenly, 'you were used to having your women take care of the precautions themselves.'

'I suppose I was.' The smile was thin. 'I'm not apologising for what I've been or done in the past. It's the future we're concerned with now. Steve's future.'

'His name is Steven,' she protested. 'I hate abbreviations!'

'Steve's a man's name,' he returned, unmoved. 'And he's a real little man.'

'He'd have to be, wouldn't he?' Her tone was bitter. 'With you for a father he wouldn't dare be anything else!'

The hand still beneath her chin tightened cruelly for a brief moment, then as swiftly relaxed again. There was a rueful line to his mouth. 'Point taken. I'm going too fast. I've a lot to learn about bringing up a child, Ria. You're going to have to lean on me hard if I take a wrong turn.'

'I haven't said I'll marry you yet,' she whispered. 'I don't even . . .'

'But you're going to.' He dropped his head and found her lips, kissing her into a state where she wasn't even sure what she had been protesting about. It was her maternal instinct that saved the day. That alone could have provided the strength both of mind and limb to push him away a second before the door opened to admit the small, pyjama-clad figure.

'I want to come in your bed,' he announced, the way he did most Wednesday mornings (how could she have forgotten that?). 'Move over, Mummy.'

He was well advanced into the room before he realised that she wasn't alone. He stopped abruptly, eyes widening, a thumb stealing up to his mouth. Ria searched her mind desperately for something to say, hating herself for allowing this to happen. Steven wasn't baby enough to accept the situation without question. He had never ever seen anyone else but her in this bed. How did she make it right for him?

The initiative was taken from her by Ty sitting up and holding out his hand. 'Come up here,' he said, smiling. 'We've got something to tell you.'

He came without obvious reluctance, kneeling up on the foot of the divan to gaze unblinkingly at the two of them. 'You remember last night asking me if I'd like to be your daddy?' said Ty, making no attempt to reach out for him. And then, receiving a barely perceptible nod in reply, 'Well, supposing I told you I really am your daddy?'

There was a pause while the statement was considered. When the reply came it wasn't what either of them was expecting to hear.

'Is that why you and Mummy were fighting?' he asked in his clear treble. 'Mummys and daddys fight a lot.'

Ty shot Ria a suddenly hardened glance. 'Where did he learn that fact of life?'

'I don't think Margaret is very selective in what she

lets him watch on television,' she said unhappily. She
held out her arms to her son, thankful when he
scampered across the bed and into them. Her nudity
was unimportant; he had seen her often enough without
clothes. What mattered was straightening out this whole
mess in his mind. 'It's true,' she murmured against his
hair. 'This is your real daddy. He's been away a long
time, but now he's come back.'

Blue-grey eyes took a quick peep. 'Is he going to live
with us?'

'Yes,' Ty stated firmly. 'We're going to be a proper
family.'

Steven was sitting up again, small face contemplative.
Suddenly he took a flying leap back to the floor, diving
out of the room before either of them could speak. He
was back while they were still looking at each other
helplessly, clutching a book to his chest.

'Read to me again,' he demanded, climbing back on
Ty's side of the mattress.

Laughter filled his father's eyes, held from bursting
forth by sheer effort of will. 'You certainly get your
priorities in the right order,' he commented, giving Ria
a thumbs-up sign behind the little boy's back. 'O.K.,
we'll read while your mother gets breakfast. That's fair,
isn't it?'

'To whom?' It was still going to be necessary to fetch
her wrap, but somehow Ria found she no longer cared.
The relief of seeing Steven curl up so confidently at Ty's
side was too great to be spoiled by minor detail. A
proper family, he had said. Dared she hope he really
meant it?

The two of them watched her across the room with
interest. She could feel both pairs of eyes on her back.

'Why aren't you wearing your nightdress, Mummy?'
asked Steven.

'Because I was too warm,' she said, tying the belt
securely about her waist.

'Were you too warm as well?' eyeing the man at his
side.

'That's it.' Ty was fighting a losing battle with brimming humour. He took refuge in the book, clearing his throat before beginning to read aloud.

Ria left them to it, heading for the kitchen with a heady lightness of step. The sun was rising into a clear blue sky. It was going to be a fine day after all the rain. They would spend it together, the three of them. She wondered if Ty had ever seen the Planetarium.

Her mood changed swiftly as memory did a double-take. It wasn't quite as simple as that, was it? What about Keith? She had more or less promised him a definite decision by the time he returned tomorrow. For more than a year she had kept him dangling on a string—her fall-back, she acknowledged ashamedly now, in case nothing better turned up. He was going to be hurt, and badly. How could she do it to him?

Except she didn't have a choice, did she? Ty wasn't going to give up his son now. If only she could feel as certain of his feelings for her. Oh, physically, yes—there was no doubting the fact that she could rouse him—but she was still a stranger to his deeper emotions. He wanted Steven; she was part of the package. Could she marry a man knowing he didn't love her?

The answer came pat. Could she not marry him knowing she would be depriving their son of his natural father?

There were eight rashers of bacon in the box. Recalling Ty's appetite, Ria grilled the lot. They hadn't eaten last night. Almost eleven hours they had spent in bed—if not exactly resting for the whole of it. It was ages since she had gone through a night without waking at least once in the small hours.

She could see the top half of her face mirrored in the bright stainless steel of the cooker trim, eyes almost indigo. The restlessness inside her had settled, satiated for the moment. Making love was a wonderful elixir. She had almost forgotten just how wonderful. Right now she felt like singing and dancing from pure exhilaration.

She had the breakfast all ready by the time her menfolk came through. Steven eyed his father's loaded plate in wonderment.

'Mummy only likes coffee and toast,' he confided, picking up his own knife and fork.

'Then Mummy had better learn new habits, and get some meat on her bones,' retorted Ty, drawing a gurgle of laughter from his son.

'I saved myself a whole rasher,' Ria informed them both in mock indignation. Her eyes sought Ty's for a moment, the warmth rising under her skin. 'I'm hungry this morning.

There was sensuality in the slow smile. 'Oddly enough, so am I. There might just be enough here to satisfy me.'

Ria hoped so. Oh, how she hoped so!

They were at the coffee stage before Ty made any reference to the rest of the day.

'What's on the agenda?' he asked. 'You don't usually spend your day off round the house, do you?'

'We're going to the Planetarium,' chimed in Steven, spraying toast crumbs. 'It's all about space!'

'Don't talk with your mouth full,' admonished Ria automatically. To Ty she added wryly, 'He's space mad!'

'I can think of worse interests. Anyway, it's been years since I was there myself.'

'You're coming with us?'

'Sure thing. I can start on the other arrangements tomorrow.'

Ria bit her lip, dropping her gaze to her plate. 'Can't it wait a few days? There are things I have to straighten out first.'

'It should only take a few minutes to issue marching orders.' His tone left little room for argument. 'I'll make sure you get them.'

Keith would be coming round as usual tomorrow evening unless she contacted him first. But she could hardly explain the situation over the telephone, could she? He deserved to hear it face to face. She dreaded the thought.

Margaret still hadn't returned when they were ready to leave the house. She had forgotten to slide the bolt last night too, Ria acknowledged. Too many other matters on her mind. It was strange to think that a mere twenty-four hours ago she hadn't even had an inkling of what was to happen. That travel programme had been pure coincidence, of course, and yet combined with Ty's choice of hers out of all the agencies in London, it became almost fatalistic.

The Planetarium entranced Steven. He was still wide-eyed with wonder when they emerged into the autumn sunshine again, chattering nineteen to the dozen about stars and moons and 'consolations'. At his special request, they had lunch at a pizza parlour, sharing a twelve-inch special with all the trimmings. So far he wasn't calling Ty anything, not even Mr Morgan. There had to be some confusion in his mind, Ria concluded, even if it wasn't evident as yet. She could only let matters take their course.

It was Ty who suggested feeding the pigeons in Trafalgar Square.

'Haven't done this since I was about eight,' he confessed, buying them each a packet of food from one of the vendors. 'From what I remember, you'd better be prepared to send that jacket of yours to the cleaners.!'

Ria was wearing a trouser suit in pale green suede that she had bought on credit from a catalogue run by one of the girls at work. She knew how well it suited her. 'It goes in the washing-machine,' she said airily. 'One thing you learn with children around is never to have anything that will spoil from a bit of dirt.'

'Seems I'm the only one at risk, then,' he said, with a disparaging glance at his dark sleeve. 'I'm going to need a change of clothes, anyway.'

'Are you staying with your mother?' Ria ventured.

'At the flat. She isn't there right now.' He swung

Steven up on to his shoulders, much to the latter's delight. 'Come on then, young un, let's get to it!'

They stayed for almost half an hour in the thronged square. Steven was in some seventh heaven, a look of pure rapture on his face as he stood surrounded, and very nearly smothered, by the greedy birds who could recognise a soft touch when they saw one. A photographer snapped the three of them together, handing over a ticket in exchange for an exorbitant sum. The prints would be posted on within a couple of days, he promised.

'Probably get "lost in the post",' was Ty's dry comment as the man moved on to find other easy prey. He glanced at his watch. 'If we go now you can be making us some tea while I change.'

Ria felt her heart lift. 'You want us to come with you?'

'Isn't that what I just said?' There was a faint irony in the line of his mouth. 'I've already told you my mother won't be there.'

Steven had moved off a few feet to finish the last of the feed. Keeping an eye on him, Ria said softly, 'What are you going to tell her about us?'

'The truth, up to a point. I can hardly explain a four-year-old son any other way.'

'How do you think she might react?'

'Predictably. You don't need to concern yourself on that score. She's what you might call a reluctant grandmother at the best—Teresa gave up trying to get her to take an interest. You'll find my sister a different proposition. She's had two children herself.'

On the right side of the blanket, Ria thought wryly. It wasn't exactly the same thing.

The Morgan residence was situated in a small, exclusive block overlooking the river. Rising to the fourth and uppermost floor in the smoothly gliding lift, Tia gave up worrying about the future in trying to come to terms with the present. She had always accepted that Ty came from a well-to-do family, but this was more than she had anticipated. Only the very rich lived in such luxurious surroundings.

If she had found the outer shell impressive, the apartment itself was even more so. Running the full length of the enormous and superbly designed living area lay a wide balcony affording magnificent views. Thick white carpet offset a colour scheme of oranges, browns and creams, with half a dozen paintings that even to Ria's untutored eye had to be orginals, strategically placed for maximum effect. The furniture itself was mostly antique, each piece individual.

'Don't touch *any*thing!' she warned Steven, who was mesmerised by the sliding glass doors which formed the balcony wall.

'He's O.K. Let him look round if he wants to.' Ty was moving across the room as he spoke, his suit jacket already off. 'I'm going to have a shower while I'm about it. If you're making tea, you might bring me a cup through.'

About to ask where the kitchen was, Ria shook herself. Seek and thou shalt find, she thought whimsically. She took Steven with her, not daring to leave him alone with so many temptations. All very well for Ty to say it; he probably didn't remember what childhood curiosity could lead to .

The kitchen was smaller than one might have anticipated for the size of the apartment. More than likely the kind of people who occupied such places rarely bothered to cook for themselves. She found some loose tea in a silver canister: Earl Grey, from the fragrant aroma. It made quite a change from tea-bags, she thought with humour, spooning the required amount into a fine Spode teapot after warming it first in the proper fashion. The cups themselves were like small soup dishes, flaring out from a narrow base. Designed for eye-appeal rather than keeping the liquid hot for very long, she calculated. She would give Ty another five minutes before taking him the promised cup. He should be out of the shower by then at least.

The sharp burr of a bell had her foxed for a moment until she realised it must be the outer door. It came again while she hesitated, uncertain whether to answer it or not. Whoever was out there might know someone was in the place, so she could hardly ignore it, yet fetching Ty through to answer it was equally out of the question.

She went on the third impatient ring, putting an eye to the peephole set into the polished wood first. One couldn't be too careful. The woman standing outside was distorted by the fish-eye lens, but her hair was certainly dark. Teresa, could it be? She seemed the most likely candidate. Ria took a steadying breath before opening the door. It had to come some time, she supposed, so why not now? A different proposition, Ty had said. She could only put her trust in his word.

CHAPTER TEN

'AND about ...' began the newcomer in aggrieved tones, breaking off abruptly when she saw who had answered the door. In the following moment's pause, Ria was aware of being swiftly and narrowly appraised. She had anticipated surprise, but was unprepared for the derisive little smile curling the other's lips.

'Well, well and well!' she drawled. 'When the cat's away the rat shows his true colours! Where is he?'

'In the shower.' Ria stood back to allow her entry. 'He shouldn't be long.'

'I'm sure.' Pale blue eyes flicked a glance along the corridor leading to the bedrooms. 'And who might you be?'

Antagonism bristling in her, Ria wished fervently that Ty would put in an appearance. There was little resemblance either in looks or manner between brother and sister. Teresa had a cover-girl beauty, her make-up flawless, her dark hair smooth and glossy. The clothes she was wearing had come from no chain store, for certain: Ria could recognise *haute couture* when she saw it.

'I'm Ria Brownlow,' she said.

The derision increased. 'Not quite what I meant, but it will do for now.' She moved on through into the living-room, casting an all-seeing glance around. 'How about getting me a drink while we wait for the lord and master?'

'You obviously know where things are kept,' Ria answered levelly. 'I'm afraid I don't.'

'No, of course not. You won't have been here before.' The other dropped her Gucci handbag on to the nearest chair and made her way across to an inlaid cabinet, opening it to reveal bottles and glasses. 'What would you like?'

135

Ty came through the door behind Ria before she could answer. He was wearing slacks and a long-sleeved casual shirt, the cuffs of which he was still in the process of fastening.

'I'm ready for . . .' he began, breaking off abruptly as his eyes fell on their visitor. For a moment his expression remained quite blank, then Ria saw a muscle tense alongside his mouth. 'I didn't hear you arrive,' he said. 'How long have you been here?'

'Just a few minutes.' The other sounded nonplussed. Whatever greeting she had been anticipating, this quite obviously wasn't it. 'Sorry if I broke something up,' she added with faint asperity. 'I was just going to have a drink. How about you?'

He shook his head. 'We're having tea.'

'Tea!' Sudden amusement coloured her tone. 'Darling, you really are a man of surprises! I suppose you'll be telling me next you don't remember our arrangement for last night?'

'I remember.' His own voice was without inflection. 'Something else cropped up.'

As if on cue, Steven appeared through an archway across the far side of the room, moving slowly with his eyes fixed on the brimming cup wobbling on the saucer he held between both hands. 'I poured you some tea, Daddy,' he announced.

Ria's breath caught in her throat. Ty was the first to move, going to meet the boy and take the cup from him. 'Thanks,' he said. 'That's just what I wanted.' He put cup and saucer down on the nearest surface, then bent to swing the small figure up in his arms, turning to face the two watching. So close together, the resemblance between them was so acute it made Ria's heart ache. 'I'd like you to meet my wife and son,' he said clearly. 'Ria—Maxine Duncan.'

The relief of finding that this was not after all Ty's sister crowded everything else from Ria's mind for a moment. It was the other woman's stunned expression that brought full realisation. She looked swiftly at Ty, meeting enigmatic grey eyes. Whatever his thoughts right now he was revealing little.

Maxine herself was slow in recovering. If she had any doubts as to the veracity of the statement, one glance at man and child was all it took to confirm at least that part of it.

'I don't understand,' she got out at last. 'There was never any mention . . . I mean, you didn't . . .'

'It's a long story,' he said on a note which suggested he was not about to go into it. 'Sorry I couldn't let you know about last night.'

'Does Denise know about this?' demanded Maxine.

'No,' he acknowledged. 'As a matter of fact, you're the first.'

'Quite an honour.' She was fast recovering from the shock—or at least pretending to. 'How do you think she's likely to take it?'

His smile was cynical. 'Like a trooper. She isn't due back until tomorrow, so that gives me twenty-four hours to work out the best way of telling her the news. Any suggestions?'

The crimson mouth hardened a fraction. 'The suggestion I have in mind you wouldn't care for,' she retorted with irony. 'I think I'd better go.' The glance she gave Ria would have frozen a polar bear. 'Very amusing, *Miss Brownlow*! I hope you'll all be very happy.'

Ty made no attempt to see her to the door. He let Steven down to the floor again as the latter started wriggling, gently smoothing the dark head.

'You told her your name?' he asked, looking across at Ria.

'Yes.' She made a small, helpless gesture. 'How was I to know what you were going to say?'

'You couldn't.' He smiled again, shaking his head. 'I didn't even know myself until it came out. It seemed the easiest way.'

'Won't it be a bit difficult to explain to your mother?'

'No more than anything else. It's going to be true enough shortly, anyway.'

They were still standing yards apart, neither making any move. Ria said thickly, 'I've turned your life inside out for you, haven't I?'

Steven tugged at his trouser-leg, face indignant. 'You didn't drink your tea!'

'Just going to,' his father assured him. He picked up the cup and saucer again, ignoring the heat ring clearly showing up on the polished wood. 'Supposing you fetch your mother one, too.'

'I'll get it,' Ria put in hastily with visions of another teetering journey across the carpet. 'It won't take me a minute.'

'There's sure to be some orange juice or something in the fridge for Steven,' Ty called after her.

There was. Ria poured a small quantity into a glass, then half filled a cup with tea for herself. She didn't feel like drinking at all, but it was something to do while they talked. And talk they must. Steven must be found some distraction.

They were sitting together on one of the long, velvet-covered sofas when she went on through. Steven was laughing over something Ty was saying, rocking back and forth in a paroxysm of glee. Watch your shoes on the cushions, it was on the tip of Ria's tongue to say. She desisted with an effort. There were more things to think about than the possibility of a little dust on the upholstery. Maxine Duncan, for one.

Ty took one look at her face and got the message. 'Why don't you go and explore?' he suggested to Steven. 'You might even find some sweets in my bedroom if you look hard enough.

'Polo mints,' he added for Ria's benefit as the child vanished hotfoot through the door. 'Special request by my mother that I don't smoke while I'm in residence.'

'You didn't smoke heavily when I knew you,' she said. 'Just the occasional cheroot.'

'It's no more than that now, but abstinence makes

the heart grow fonder.' He shook a faintly mocking head at her weak smile. 'You can do better than that.'

'I don't feel like joking.' Ria took a seat opposite him, putting down the untouched cup on a side-table. 'We have to talk things through, Ty.'

'We've said all there is to say on the subject.'

'No, we haven't.' She paused, searching for the words. 'We haven't given ourselves the chance to really think about the long-term situation. Marriage isn't something anyone should enter into lightly.'

'I agree,' he said. 'But circumstances have to have some bearing. Steven needs a father.'

'He's managed quite adequately for four years without one,' she retorted, stung by the reply.

'He didn't have any choice, did he? You made the decision for him.'

She flushed, unable to meet the grey eyes. 'You blame me for that?'

'Of course I blame you.' His tone was suddenly harsh. 'You robbed me of his first four years. How else do you expect me to feel!'

She shook her head numbly. 'That isn't fair, Ty. How was I to guess you'd even want to know?'

'You could have given me the chance. You knew where I was. A letter might have taken a week or two to catch up with me, but I'd have been on the next plane out.'

'To suggest I got rid of it, the way my uncle and aunt wanted me to?'

'No, dammit!' Ty was sitting forward in his seat, mouth a thin angly line. 'I'm not into murdering anybody's kid, much less my own! We'd have been married five years longer, that's all—maybe had two or three by now.'

Ria looked at him then, trying not to sound sarcastic. 'You didn't come across as a potential family man at the time.'

His laugh was short. 'No doubt I still don't. If you'd asked me five years back if I had any yearning to produce I'd have said, no way. Only saying it is one thing, meaning it is something else. I'd never met any woman I'd have wanted to have a kid by, that's about what it boils down to. You were the first decent . . .' He broke off, shrugging broad shoulders. 'It's immaterial now, isn't it? Regrets don't turn any clocks back. Considering the time element, it's going to be Monday at the earliest. That gives me the weekend to introduce you to the family.'

Ria fought the sudden rising sense of panic. 'As soon as that?'

'There's no reason to wait.' He added expressionlessly, 'You didn't want a church wedding, did you?'

'No,' she admitted. 'Not in these circumstances.'

'Then why the reluctance? We owe it to Steven to make him legitimate at the first possible opportunity.'

And what then? she wanted to ask, but the words wouldn't come. Instead she said haltingly, 'I still have to tell Keith.'

There was no discernible reaction. 'Is he likely to turn nasty?'

'Oh, no! He's not the type. He's . . .' she lifted her shoulders in a wry little gesture, 'going to be very hurt.'

'I can imagine, but it has to be done.' The pause was brief. 'Unless you'd prefer me to do the telling for you?'

'That would be even worse!' She hesitated before tagging on slowly, 'We never slept together.'

'I realise that.' His tone was even. 'It's possible to tell when a woman hasn't had sexual relations for a long time. Having a child around must have limited your social life all the way through.'

'I don't regret it,' she denied. 'He's worth more to me than any man!'

'I can believe it.' If the sting had penetrated, Ty still wasn't revealing it.

Excluding you, she almost added, only she knew it wasn't wholly true. If it came to a choice between Ty and their son, she would choose Steven every time. A mother could do no other.

'I really think we should be getting back,' she said. 'Margaret will be wondering what happened to us. We're not usually out past four o'clock on a Wednesday.'

'Fine by me,' he agreed. 'I'll get my things. Those disposable razors you use are O.K. on occasion, but I prefer my own old trusty.'

'You're coming with us?'

Dark brows rose. 'You'd rather I didn't?'

'Of course not. I mean, naturally I want you to . . .' Ria broke off, torn between conflicting emotions. 'What do I tell Margaret?' she concluded unhappily.

'The truth. What else? She's going to have to know sooner or later. You won't be staying there for very much longer.'

Ria hadn't thought that far ahead. She didn't particularly want to now. One thing at a time; they weren't even married yet.

They took a taxi from door to door. Steven chattered non-stop all the way. On reaching the house, he darted into Margaret's domain before Ria could stop him. They could hear his excited, breathless voice as he attempted to impart the day's impressions, with 'Daddy' the word most in use. Ria looked at Ty with rueful acceptance.

'I suppose we'd better go and straighten things out.'

Margaret was in the kitchen, looking both bewildered and bemused as she listened to the outpourings. Her expression, on seeing that Ria herself was not alone, became even more so.

'I'm sorry,' she said. 'I didn't realise you had a visitor or I'd have come straight out.'

'Margaret, I'd like you to meet Steven's father,' said Ria clearly. 'Ty Morgan—Margaret Wright.'

'Short for Tyler?' asked the other, obviously at a loss for anything else to say.

Ty laughed. 'Even worse—Tyson.'

'I didn't know that.' Ria flushed as she caught Margaret's eye. 'We never knew each other all that well,' she added with soul-destroying honesty.

'A matter that's about to be rectified,' Ty cut in smoothly. 'We're going to be married as soon as it can be arranged.'

The older woman gave him a level look. 'Better late than never, I suppose.'

'You don't understand . . .' began Ria, then stopped as Ty shook his head.

'There's a lot of truth in that,' he said. 'We can't replace five years but we can try making up for them. From what Ria tells me, you've been very good to her and Steven. I'm grateful.'

'I only did what any decent person would do.' She was still holding back. Her glance went to the small overnight case in his hand. 'You're staying?'

'If that's all right with you.'

'It's entirely up to Ria. I don't interfere in her private life.'

'Ty knows about Keith,' Ria hastened to assure her. 'I'll be telling him tomorrow.'

'He's going to be very upset,' said Margaret with some understatement. 'But I suppose you know what you're doing.' She rallied with an effort. 'Would you like some tea?'

'Thanks, but we've already had some,' Ty responded easily. 'Sorry we had to spring this on you, and I hope you'll come to the wedding—perhaps even act as witness?'

'Well, I don't know about that.' Despite herself, she was beginning to unbend. 'I really don't know.'

'Think about it,' he advised. 'It's going to be next week for sure, although I'm not certain yet which day. Depends when they can fit us in at the register office.'

'You won't be getting wed in church, then?'

He smiled, glance going to Steven who was playing on the floor with Clancy. 'Not really feasible, is it?'

A sigh and a shake of the greying head signalled recognition. 'Good luck to you both, anyway,' she added with restraint. 'I hope it all turns out for the best.'

She wasn't alone in that, thought Ria on the way upstairs. All very well to talk about giving Steven a name he could call his own, but there was a lot more to consider too.

Steven was in the bath when he finally voiced the question Ria had been half expecting all day.

'Mummy,' he said thoughtfully, 'if Mr Morgan is my real daddy why haven't I seen him before?'

Anticipated though the question was, the answer was no less difficult. 'He didn't know about you,' she said.

'Why?'

'Because I didn't tell him you'd been born.'

His forehead puckered. 'Would he have come sooner if you'd told him?'

'Oh, yes.' She said it as if she really believed it. 'Straight away, darling! It's all my fault that he didn't.'

'Never mind, Mummy.' Wet little arms slid around her neck in a rare and comforting little hug as she knelt at the bathside. 'He's here now.'

And that was the most important thing, Ria conceded. If Steven himself could accept it she could do no less.

Ty came in to read the story already booked by his son as soon as the latter was tucked into bed. Ria said her good nights first and left them to it. There were some lamb chops in the fridge that she had been saving for tomorrow night. Smothered in mushrooms, onions and a thick tomato sauce and served with rice plus what other vegetables she could turn up, they should make an adequate enough meal. For dessert they could make do with cheese and biscuits.

She had the casserole in the oven and the table ready set by the time Ty came back through. He looked surprised to find her so busy.

'So this is why you disappeared so fast,' he remarked. 'I though maybe a spot of resentment might be involved.'

Blue eyes met grey. 'Because you're the one he

wants reading to him these days? I'm not that petty-minded, Ty.'

'It wouldn't be unnatural under the circumstances.' His tone was level. 'I can't take your place, Ria. I can only make my own.'

'I know. And I told you, I don't resent it.' She paused briefly. 'You did want some dinner, didn't you?'

He laughed. 'There's nothing wrong with my appetite, and something is already starting to smell delicious! You always could cook. I can still remember that chilli you made the night I agreed to take you with us to Sibu. I haven't tasted one to better it since.'

Ria could remember it too; she could remember a lot of things. She said diffidently, 'It's nothing out of the ordinary. I don't even have a bottle of wine in to go with it.'

'I'll slip out and fetch one,' he offered. 'Assuming there's an off-licence somewhere close-ish.'

'About five minutes' walk,' she acknowledged. 'If you're sure you don't mind?'

'Look,' he said, 'let's stop acting like polite strangers, shall we? That's *our* son through there. If for no other reason, we owe him the effort. I'll fetch the wine, you make the meal and afterwards . . .' he paused, mouth tilting a little, 'well, we'll let that take care of itself.'

Which it would, Ria had no doubt. The very thought of being in Ty's arms again thrilled her. It was emotionally that she felt so confused, one minute believing herself in love with him again, the next almost hating him. She had lied when she denied all resentment where Steven's feelings were concerned. Her son was no longer all hers. If this marriage of theirs was going to have any chance of success she had to learn to share. After all these years that wasn't going to be easy.

A shared bottle of St Emilion went a long way towards relaxing the atmosphere. Ty insisted she leave the clearing away until later, pouring out the last of the wine to drink with their coffee in lieu of a brandy as they sat before the gas fire.

'It's been a long time since I spent an evening like this,' he commented lazily, lying back against the sofa cushions. 'Good food, good wine and a lovely woman—what more could any man ask!'

'Who exactly is Maxine Duncan?' asked Ria softly.

He sighed. 'I thought it was too good to last. Is she important?'

'You tell me.'

'The short answer is no, but I don't suppose you're going to be satisfied with that.'

'Not really.' Ria was looking at the glass in her hand, watching the ruby contents glow in the firelight as she turned it. 'She's very beautiful.'

'She's also a bitch.'

'It didn't stop you . . . dating her.'

'You were going to say sleeping with her.' He sounded rueful. 'Not easy to pull the wool over your eyes, is it? Why?' He shrugged. 'I was at a loose end and she made herself available. What more can I say?'

Ria had changed her mind because she had genuinely preferred not to know. She would still have preferred it. She said tautly, 'In other words, you used her.'

'No more than she used me. Twice married, twice divorced and with an eye open for the main chance—that's Maxine.'

'And you were it?'

The wince was not wholly theatrical. 'I suppose I asked for that one. Would it do any good to point out that I hadn't found you again when I made that arrangement for last night?'

'But you finished up in bed with me instead, so you didn't lose out.'

Ty turned his head to look at her, brows drawn together. 'I'm not apologising for anything that happened before yesterday lunchtime, Ria. If it happened again, then you'd have some cause for complaint.'

'You're saying it won't?' She shook her head as he opened his mouth to reply. 'Ty, you've been used to complete freedom in that department. You're thirty-seven. You're not going to alter your habits now.'

'You could try giving me the chance,' he responded after a moment. 'Try having a little faith in yourself too. You satisfy me.'

For the moment, she thought. But what about later, when the novelty of having a wife had worn off? After the kind of life he had led these past years, it was going to be hard for him to settle to a regular routine. Family contacts might find him a job, but could he hold one down? He would have to sell his boat, for one thing. That wasn't going to be easy. They wouldn't be living here in the flat according to what he had intimated. That left the question wide open.

He reached out and took the glass from her hand while she was still searching for a way to ask, drawing her to him to kiss her long and hard on the mouth.

'You're not like the others,' he murmured fiercely against her lips. 'You never were! Trust me, Ria.'

She wanted to. Oh, how she wanted to! She could feel herself melting, the stress dissolving into a different kind of tension as her whole body began to come alive under his skilful caresses. Fingers trembling, she unfastened his shirt, pressing her lips to his chest where the whorls of dark hair curled damply. His skin tasted faintly salty, emitting an erotic and wholly masculine scent. Her hands traced the shape of his rib cage, clearly defined beneath the layer of muscle, sliding around his waist to run lightly over the broad back. She could hear his roughened breathing, feel the strong beat of his heart. Her own was pounding in her throat, in her ears, catching her up in its delirium.

'I think we should go to bed,' said Ty gruffly. 'There's no cover here if Steven walks in on us.'

Ria lifted her head, trying to read his expression. 'Do you find that an annoyance?'

'No,' he returned, 'it's just a parental precaution.

When he's old enough to start asking the questions I'll supply the answers, but I'm no progressive when it comes to personal privacy.' He kissed her again, hands curving her face, his smile warming. 'At least we lasted a couple of hours longer than last night. Bed at ten doesn't sound nearly as degenerate as eight!'

'As if,' she laughed back as he lifted her to her feet, 'it would bother you one iota!'

The bed was lacking a second occupant when Ria awoke at seven. It took the sight of his things still lying across the chair where he had tossed them the night before to reassure her that he hadn't had a change of mind and crept out on her in the early hours.

Not that it was likely after the night they had spent, she acknowledged, relaxing back into the pillows for a moment or two. He had been so tender, so infinitely caring. If he hadn't said the actual words themselves, he had to feel something deeper than mere physical need to behave like that. Her own emotions were in no doubt. She loved him so desperately it hurt. Sharing Steven no longer seemed a problem. Ty was going to make a wonderful father. Perhaps next time they might manage a daughter—although another boy would be delightful too. She stretched luxuriously. Next time she would no longer be alone. That one fact in itself meant everything to her.

Last night's dishes had been washed and put away when she got through to the kitchen. Wearing the short silk robe he had brought with him, Ty was reading the paper while he drank coffee from a freshly percolated pot.

'Just don't expect me to make a habit of it,' he growled with mock severity when she thanked him.

'Uncle Keith didn't wash up when he was here,' piped up Steven, ear bent to listen to the snap, crackle and pop of his breakfast cereal as he poured on milk. 'He said it wasn't a man's job.'

'He stayed the night a couple of times when the

weather turned bad,' Ria explained hastily, catching
Ty's glance. 'He slept on the sofa.'

Ty accepted the latter statement without comment.
'A man should be able to turn his hand to anything,' he
said to his son on a mild note. 'There's nothing
demeaning about keeping a tidy ship.'

Steven considered the advice, head on one side.
'What does demeaning mean?' he asked, stumbling
slightly over the long word.

'Undignified,' supplied Ria. 'Uncle Keith doesn't
have enough confidence in himself, that's all.' She bit
her lip, realising how true that was, in more ways than
one. Telling him about Ty was going to be one of the
hardest things she had ever been called on to do in her
life. Only there was no choice, was there? If she didn't
do it tonight, Ty would do it for her—and he was
hardly likely to be gentle about it. 'Eat your cereal,' she
added rather more brusquely than she had intended.
'We're going to be late.'

Ty said nothing; the narrowed line of his mouth was
enough. Ria could appreciate his feelings. In similar
circumstances she was sure she would feel just the same.
Keith had known his son longer than he had. The fact
that he had never in all that time got as close was
unlikely to register. The sooner she had the whole
straightened out, the better for all concerned—Keith
included. He was young enough to find himself another
wife. She couldn't spend the rest of her life feeling sorry
for something she couldn't help.

'I'm taking it you'll want me to leave Steven with
Margaret today?' she asked after a moment or two
during which no one uttered a word.

'It might be best,' Ty agreed. 'I'm going to be
doing a lot of running around, with one thing and
another.'

He sounded curt. Ria avoided looking at him. 'Are
you coming back here later?' she ventured.

'It's doubtful. You'll need a clear field.'

That brought her head round. 'Ty . . .'

'Leave it,' he advised. 'I don't really want to know any more. I'll meet you from work tomorrow.'

Thirty-six hours before she saw him again—*if* she saw him again. She still couldn't convince herself that this marriage of theirs was ever going to take place.

CHAPTER ELEVEN

MARGARET was restrained in her greeting, although not with Steven himself.

'Ty's not leaving with you?' she asked.

'Probably in about half an hour,' Ria told her, judging how long it might take him to shave and shower. 'You don't mind him staying on?'

'I already told you, the flat is yours. If he was just a man you'd brought home for the night it might be a different matter, but I'd hardly object to Steven's father.' She hesitated, searching Ria's face. 'Are you quite sure you know what you're doing? It's been a long time.'

'My own fault,' she admitted wryly. 'I should have contacted him before.'

'You think he'd have come?'

Ria sighed suddenly and shrugged. 'I'm never really likely to know, am I? He's here now, that's what counts.' She added impulsively, 'I hope you will stand for us as witness, Margaret. I can't think of anyone I'd rather have.'

'It depends when it's going to be.' There was another brief pause and a change of tone. 'I suppose you'll be leaving here once it's all over?'

'Not without adequate notice.'

'That's the least of my worries. I can afford to let the place stand empty till I find somebody else suitable.' Her glance went to Steven, already involved with a box of lettered bricks. 'I'll miss him.'

'You'll see plenty of him,' Ria promised, drawing shrewd eyes back to her face.

'You'll be staying here in England, then?'

'Oh, yes.' She closed her mind to any faint doubt. 'I'm not sure where we'll be living yet, but there's no question of going anywhere else. There's Steven's schooling, for one thing.'

'Children get educated all over the world,' came the dry response. 'Still, you know what you want.'

Yes, thought Ria with certainty, she did. A settled home, a secure future for Steven, that had to come before anything else. If Ty couldn't provide it then she would have to think again.

She kept her own counsel where the people at the office were concerned. There would be time enough, she told herself, to let them in on the news when the wedding was actually arranged. She could always change her day off if necessary. One more subject she and Ty were going to need to discuss was her job. With Steven due to start full-time school after Christmas, she could perhaps convert to part-time hours. Not that money should be any problem if Ty sold the boat. It was just that she would prefer to retain some measure of independence.

The proposed meeting with his family bothered her almost as much as the coming interview with Keith. With any luck he would acquaint them with the facts in time to allow for some adjustment on their part before the weekend itself. Just where it would take place was something else again. She only hoped it wouldn't be at his mother's apartment with all the attendant risks of Steven having some mishap. Denise Morgan sounded the last kind of person to show any real tolerance where small boys were concerned. A reluctant grandmother, Ty had called her. It didn't exactly inspire confidence.

She was home by six-fifteen and had Steven in bed before seven, much to his disgust. Keith would be expecting dinner as usual; she could scarcely do less than prepare a meal for the two of them. How she was going to broach the subject she hadn't yet decided. A blunt announcement seemed so cruel, yet leading up to it gently seemed equally difficult.

She was still vacillating when she let him in, holding up her face automatically for his kiss before realising what she was doing.

'I've done over twenty thousand in a couple of days!' he enthused, brandishing a bottle. 'Thought we might celebrate.' He glanced round, face falling a little. 'Steven in bed already?'

'He was tired,' Ria claimed, remembering the struggle she had had explaining why his father wasn't available to tuck him in tonight. In two short days Ty had become the hub of his young life. God help them both if he let them down now.

'I brought him a present.' Keith took a small, wrapped parcel from his pocket. 'It's nothing much, just a Matchbox car for his collection. He can have it in the morning.'

Ria took the parcel from him, throat hurting. 'That was thoughtful of you.'

'I'm hoping,' he added softly, 'that we'll have more than one thing to celebrate tonight, Ria. Have you come to a decision yet?'

'Yes.' When it came right down to it, she thought numbly, the choice had been made for her. She half turned away, unable to look him in the eye. 'I think you'd better sit down, Keith. There's a lot I have to tell you.'

'If you want more time, that's O.K. by me,' he hastened to tag on, following her lead.

'I've taken too much already,' she said wryly. 'It isn't fair of me, and I'm sorry. I realise an apology is totally inadequate, of course. It's . . .'

'You don't have anything to apologise for.' His expression was downcast. 'I know I'm no great catch. I just . . .'

'You don't understand,' she cut in. 'I'm not saying no because I don't think enough of you, Keith. Something happened while you were away. Something totally unexpected.' She paused, still not sure how to say it. In the end there was only the one way. 'Steven's father turned up. It was pure chance that we happened to meet. He came in to book a flight back east. He was as surprised as I was. He asked me to have lunch with

him, just to talk over old times, then in the evening he
followed me back here. That's when he saw Steven.' She
was explaining too much too fast, but she couldn't seem
to stop the words tumbling out. 'I never let him know,
you see. He was as much in the dark as you've been.
You were always so good about not asking too many
questions, Keith. You just accepted the fact that I'd had
an affair and been left in the lurch. But it wasn't like
that. It wasn't Ty's fault.'

Keith said dully, 'You're trying to tell me he wants
you back after all this time?'

'Yes.' Her hands were twisting unconsciously together. 'We're going to be married as soon as he can
organise it, so that Steven can take his name.'

'Only for that reason?'

'No.' She hoped she was right about that. 'He wants
me, too.'

'And obviously you want him.' He was silent for a
moment, struggling to conceal his deeper feelings. 'You
must have loved him very much all those years ago for
it to last this long.'

'It wasn't so much a case of lasting as being
resurrected,' she admitted. 'I hadn't thought about him
for ages until that programme on Monday evening. We
were in Borneo at the time, you see.'

'So that's why you went so quiet.' He eyed her
reflectively. 'I'd like to meet him.'

Ria looked at him sharply. 'Do you really think
that's a good idea?'

'I don't know. I only know I'd like to meet him,' he
repeated with uncustomary stubbornness. 'I think I
merit that much.'

She spread her hands in a helpless little gesture. 'I
don't see any point, but if it's what you want. How
about tomorrow night?'

'He'll be here?'

Once again Ria could only place her trust in her
hopes. 'Yes, he'll be here. He's taking us to meet his
family over the weekend.'

'That should be an experience for you all.' Keith got to his feet, shaking his head as she made a movement to rise with him. 'No, I'd rather see myself out. I have a lot to think about.'

Ria waited until he was at the door before saying in a small voice, 'I really am sorry, Keith. I've treated you abominably.'

'Not true. You gave me a wonderful year.' His head was bowed; he didn't turn. 'See you tomorrow, then.'

She sat for a long time after he had gone, the lonely evening stretching ahead. One more thing to anticipate with dread, yet she could hardly have refused the request. Ty's reaction she hesitated to guess. He was far from predictable on any score.

There was no sign of him when she left the office at five-thirty the following day. She made her way home in a fog of depression which gave way to bitterness when she was forced to make up excuses for his continued absence to her son. The least he could have done was telephoned.

His arrival scarcely half an hour behind her elicited delight on Steven's part but left her cold and furious and ready to reject any excuse out of hand.

'I suppose you're going to tell me you couldn't get through on the phone!' she stormed, for once ignoring Steven's presence.

'I'm not going to try telling you anything till you've calmed down,' he retorted with a meaningful glance in their son's direction. 'You sound like a fishwife!'

'I'm nobody's wife yet,' she said, taking a hold on herself. 'If you can break one promise you can break another.'

'I was caught in a traffic jam,' he came back with control. 'Difficult to reach a phone from the back of a taxi. If you'd given me a few minutes' leeway there'd have been no problem.'

The anger died out of her suddenly. Lower lip caught

between her teeth, she looked away. 'Keith's coming round to meet you,' she said indistinctly.

'Why?' The control was still there but underlaid with sharpness.

'He asked, that's why. I can't read his mind.'

'Then he's going to be unlucky, because I don't want to meet him.'

'You have to.' She was trying hard not to appeal. 'I can't call it off now.'

'You shouldn't have arranged it in the first place.'

'I didn't. At least ...' she paused, lifting her shoulders, 'is it really so important?'

'It's unnecessary.' There was no softening of tone. 'You haven't even asked me how I got on yesterday.'

They were still standing, barely feet apart in distance, several miles separate in understanding. Steven watched the two of them, a thumb in his mouth and an anxious expression on his face. Ria forced herself to smile, to relax her stance. If only for Steven's sake, they had to stop this now.

'So tell me,' she invited.

Whatever his faults, petulance was not among them. He said evenly, 'It's set for Wednesday at eleven-thirty. I booked a table at Langham's for lunch—just the two of us. Margaret is going to bring Steven back here with her.'

Ria blinked. 'When did you organise that?'

'Just now when she let me in downstairs.' His smile lacked humour. 'I think she's beginning to see me in a slightly better light.'

Ria wished she could say the same. She felt so much at odds with herself, so overwrought. Thinking about marrying Ty was one thing, doing it quite another. She had been on her own for too long. Did she really want to share her life with anyone when it came down to it?

But it wasn't just her life, was it? There was Steven to consider. These past couple of days had proved how much he needed a father figure. She had to go through with it now, and make the best of it.

'It's about your bedtime,' she said, looking across at the silent child.

'No, let him stay for a while.' Ty grinned as the sober young face lit up. 'How about showing me your train set? I haven't played engine drivers in years!'

Don't try taking over from me! Ria wanted to shout at him, but she bit it back. There was going to be no emotional tug of war, with Steven pulled this way and that between sparring parents. She and Ty would have to reach an understanding with regard to rules and regulations, but out of Steven's hearing.

Father and son were both kneeling on the floor engrossed in the wide gauge track and plastic rolling-stock when the front door bell rang at seven-thirty.

'That will be Keith,' said Ria stonily when Ty failed to react. 'What do I tell him?'

Grey eyes lifted for a brief, expressionless moment. 'Let him come up if it means so much to you. It's no skin off my nose.'

So wasn't that what she had wanted? she asked herself ruefully as she went to answer the summons. Or wasn't it truer to say it was only Ty's opposition that had sparked off the whole futile argument? There was no point in this meeting—not for any of them.

Keith looked immaculate in his best grey suit. He also looked resolute. Ty was still on the floor when they got upstairs. He rose as they entered, dusting off the knees of his pale beige slacks with a careless hand. Ria murmured unnecessary introductions, aware of the total dissimilarity in type as the two men briefly shook hands. Ty was several inches taller and appeared even broader than usual beside Keith's slighter build.

'I just wanted to wish you luck,' said the latter, sounding hollow and uncomfortable. 'And to say there's no ill-feeling so far as I'm concerned. Ria and Steven's happiness is all I care about.'

One dark brow acquired a sardonic tilt. 'They'll be well taken care of.'

'Oh, I'm sure.' The disclaimer was hasty.

Apart from a distracted greeting, Steven had paid little attention to the newcomer. Now he tugged urgently at his father's trouser-leg. 'Daddy, the train can't leave the station without a driver!'

'Better pack it away for now,' advised Ty kindly but firmly. 'We'll run down to Land's End another day.'

There was no argument on the child's part, although he was obviously disappointed. Ria said swiftly, 'How about a drink?'

'Why not?' Ty went to do the honours, underlining his authority in a way that left little room for doubt. He poured three measures of whisky, added twice the volume in soda to one of them, then hovered with a finger on the syphon plunger while he glanced in Keith's direction. 'Straight?'

The younger man nodded, accepting the glass with a faintly sheepish expression on his face. Ria avoided his eyes; it was enough for him to know he had lacked the confidence to be his own man without driving the lesson home. Guilt speared her through. She had put him in this position. She should have made last night a final and unequivocal farewell.

Conversation limped along while Steven finished clearing away his train set. Ria for one was heartily relieved when Keith made a move to break up the gathering after finishing off the undiluted whisky in a couple of forced swallows.

'I have an appointment near here at eight,' he said. 'Whole-life policy, if I'm lucky.' He appeared on the verge of offering his hand to Ty again, then obviously thought better of it, making it a nod instead. 'Like I said, all the best.'

Steven waved a cheerful hand in answer to the proffered goodbye. 'Bye, Uncle Keith.' And then in sudden recollection, 'Thank you for the car.'

Ria accompanied him down to the front door. 'I'm sorry,' she said lamely. 'I really am, Keith.'

'Not your fault.' His tone was rueful. 'I shouldn't have come.'

She looked at him a moment, blue eyes vivid. 'Why did you?'

'I'm not all that sure now,' he admitted. 'Perhaps I hoped . . .' He paused, his smile sudden and wry. 'No, I'll be honest. I thought he'd be one of those fly-by-night types who'd let you down again first chance he got, and I wanted you to realise I'd be ready to pick up the pieces when it happened.'

The irritation she felt was unfair, she knew, yet she still wanted to shake him. 'You've got to live your own life,' she said, 'and forget about me.'

'I shall now. Or at least, I'll make some attempt.' He added diffidently, 'It's some consolation to know you're in good hands. He obviously thinks the world of Steven.'

Of Steven, yes, but what of her? thought Ria numbly as she closed the door on his departing back. Would she ever know how it felt to be secure in Ty's love?

He was running the bath when she got back upstairs, shirt-sleeves rolled ready for action. Steven squealed as he was grabbed and dumped bodily into the warm water, but it was from excitement not fear. They neither of them appeared to be missing her in any way, so she didn't interfere, going on through to the kitchen where she began preparing a meal with tears prickling the backs of her eyes.

Stupid to be jealous of a natural affinity, she told herself ashamedly. She should be thankful that Ty felt the way he did about their son. A boy and his father enjoyed a very special relationship, one which in no way affected his love for and need of a mother. She would still be the one he turned to for comfort when he was hurt or sick or simply ready for a little spoiling. Could she really begrudge him the rest?

Ty came in while she was stirring the soup heating on one of the burners. 'I'll watch that for you,' he offered. 'Steven's waiting for you to say good night.'

She went without a word to find the child already tucked up in bed, cheeks rosy and glowing. His hug was warm and unrestrained.

'I love you, too,' he murmured as usual in the nightly ritual. 'And Daddy.' His eyes were almost closed. 'You love Daddy as well, don't you, Mummy?'

'Yes,' she whispered huskily. 'Of course I do.'

She was quiet over the meal. Ty made little attempt to draw her out of it. Only when they had finished dessert and were waiting for the coffee to finish perking did he finally bring the subject into the open.

'I'm not trying to take him away from you,' he said evenly. 'It's about time you started seeing things my way for a change. Making up for lost time, it's called. O.K., so maybe I wouldn't have found him quite so fascinating when he was a baby and needed feeding and changing, etcetera. I'm not that domesticated. Only for God's sake stop looking as if you've been kicked every time he shows the slightest preference for my company!'

Ria's head was down, a hard lump in her throat. 'I didn't realise it showed so much,' she muttered.

'Well, it does. And it's giving me the pip. He's not your kid or my kid, he's *ours*!'

Her head jerked, eyes flashing. 'You don't need to shout!'

'I didn't even get started.' His face was tense, mouth a thin line. 'I'm doing my level best to put things right for all of us, and you're not helping.'

'Oh, I'm sorry. I forgot to tell you how grateful I was!'

'The thing you should be grateful for,' he grated, 'is that I didn't kick your fancy man right back down those stairs tonight! What the hell did you think you were going to gain by sticking him under my nose like that?'

It was an apt remark, came the fleeting thought. Keith had just about come level with his upper lip!

'You laugh in my face,' Ty threatened, catching the involuntary little smile, 'and you'll not sit down for a week!'

'Oh, stop it,' Ria said wearily. 'I'm no more impressed by the he-man tactics than I was five years

ago. I wasn't laughing at you, I was smiling because
. . .' She broke off, suddenly too miserable to bother
finding the right words. 'It doesn't matter. You
wouldn't understand.'

'I don't understand you,' he said after a moment or
two, tone flat and unemotional. 'Not any more. What
happened to the girl I used to know?'

'I answered that once already,' she responded. 'She
grew up. With a vengeance, you might say. I'll get the
coffee.'

He was on his feet before her, moving to intercept her.
'You're not going anywhere until we get this sorted out.'

'There's nothing to sort out,' Ria denied. 'The
wedding has been arranged. What more is there?'

Ty studied her narrowly. 'You're having doubts?'

'Of course I'm having doubts.' She groped blindly for
a chair back, using it as a prop. 'It's been too long, Ty.
We hardly know each other any more.'

'We hardly knew each other five years ago,' he said.
'Would you have married me then if I'd asked you?'

'That's a futile . . .'

'Would you?' he insisted.

Ria shrugged. 'All right, then, yes.'

'Why?'

'Because I was crazy about you.' The mockery was
aimed at herself not at him. 'Like you said, a silly little
romantic.'

'I never called you silly. I never even thought it.' His
tone had lost the rough edge. 'We're starting from the
same basis, Ria, with Steven as incentive. Give it a
chance.'

She gazed at him, eyes veiled, wishing he would stop
talking and pull her into his arms the way he had done
that first night. It might not be love but it could be a
substitute. 'I don't really have much choice, do I?' she
said at length. 'Steven already looks on you as his
father. Now can I get that coffee?'

'Sure.' Lips twisting, he stood back. 'Make mine
black.'

So what had she expected? Ria asked herself numbly as she went through to the kitchen. Ty hadn't pretended five years ago and he wasn't going to start now. He was doing this for Steven, no one else. The fact that he could still enjoy making love to her was a bonus no doubt, but it was his son who held the key to his heart. Give it a chance, he had said. Two days wasn't much of a one, was it? Not for either of them.

He was sitting in one of the armchairs gazing into the gas flames when she returned with the tray. Ria set down the latter carefully before looking across at him with a faint wry smile.

'I was being juvenile,' she said. 'We're doing the right thing.'

'Let's hope so,' Ty responded heavily. 'For all our sakes.'

They drank the coffee in near silence. It was left to Ria to make a determined effort to get things back on a proper footing again.

'I'll have to inform Mr Hardy at the office,' she said on a practical note. 'I'll see about it tomorrow.'

Ty looked up sharply. 'You're not planning on going in tomorrow?'

'Of course I am. It's the busiest day of the week.'

He studied her a moment, his gaze hardening again. 'You mean you haven't told them yet?'

Ria made a defensive gesture. 'Told them what? I didn't even know myself until tonight.'

'Only the actual day was in doubt.'

'Was it?' She had flushed but she held his gaze. 'I was hardly going to start spreading the news around on the basis of a vague promise.'

'It was never vague, and you knew it!' He was sitting up straight, body tensed. 'What in hell's name else was I supposed to do?'

Tell me you love me, she thought bitterly. Even if it wasn't true. Aloud she said, 'Trust grows, Ty, it doesn't come automatically. You could have changed your mind. You still could.'

'There's no chance of it. Not from my side. If there are any second thoughts around,' he added harsly, '*you're* the one who's having them!'

'It's all happening so fast,' she said. 'In four days my whole life has altered. Is it surprising I'm finding it difficult to adjust?'

'If I can do it,' he responded, 'so can you. We're supposed to be going out to my sister's place in Essex tomorrow. My mother is going to be there too.'

'You told them?'

'I told my mother last night. She'll have passed on the news by now.'

Blue eyes searched grey, discovering little. 'How did she take it?'

The strong mouth curved mirthlessly. 'Not without comment. Don't worry about it—she adjusts fast to any situation. Anyway, that's not the issue.'

'I can't take tomorrow off,' Ria repeated stubbornly. 'Not just like that. We can go on Sunday, can't we?'

'Seems we'll have to.' He was making an obvious effort to be reasonable. 'I'll phone through and rearrange it.' There was a pause before he tagged on slowly, 'About your job, Ria . . .'

'We can talk about that later, can't we?' she said, unwilling to disturb the uneasy peace. 'There are so many other things to think about—such as where we're going to live, for one. I don't suppose Margaret would have any objection to our staying on here until we decide.'

The look he gave her held an element of calculation. 'Why not? I'll be able to relieve her of looking after Steven for the day tomorrow, at any rate.'

'Where will you take him?' asked Ria, stifling the swift pang.

'Haven't thought about it yet.' If he was aware of her reaction he wasn't revealing it either. 'Depends what the weather's like.' He finished his coffee, glancing her way again with altered expression. 'Why don't you come over here?'

Against all inclinations, she held her ground. 'If you want me,' she said, '*you* come over *here*.'

The slow smile mocked her childish resistance. 'It makes no difference providing we finish up in the same place.'

Which they would, there was no doubt in her mind on that score. At the very least, she thought wryly, there was reassurance in his lovemaking.

Sunday was one of those brilliant Indian summer days that sometimes take the year by surprise. Ria wore cool turquoise cotton and felt almost lighthearted as they drove out of town in the car Ty had hired for the day. Nothing that anyone could say was going to undermine her mood, she vowed privately. Come Wednesday Steven would be a Morgan by name as well as birth. No one could take that away from him.

Her first glimpse of Morlands brought a faint sense of restriction due to its imposing size and location, but she refused to give way to it. No matter how Ty's family might feel about her, he was the one she was marrying. For Steven's sake she could take anything thrown at her and come up smiling.

The sight of a child's bicycle parked by the front door of the house eased her a little. Children and bicycles suggested a home, not a showpiece. She was further reassured by the greeting issued by Ty's sister, who was waiting for them in the lovely but comfortable sitting-room. Tall and dark-haired, with calm, intelligent features, she was friendly without being gushing, obviously prepared to reserve any judgment for a future date. The mother was a different proposition altogether. From the initial, all-encompassing glance which took in both the cost and probably origin of her outfit, Ria felt weighed up and found wanting, although the woman was civil enough on the surface. She was what was termed as 'beautifully preserved', her figure in the superb Chanel suit as slender as a model's, her face expertly made up. Like her offspring, she was dark-haired, with no hint of grey revealed in the smooth and glossy styling.

'Adam took the boys to see their other grandmother,' Teresa announced. 'They'll be back for lunch. Perhaps Steven might like to see the playroom?' The last with a smile at the child. 'My two are older, but they hate throwing anything away so I'm sure there'll be something in there you'll like.' She held out a hand. 'I'll show you, shall I?'

Somewhat to Ria's surprise, he went off quite happily. Ty looked as if he would as soon have gone with him, but restrained himself. Mrs Morgan allowed her glance to pass from one to the other with equal disparagement.

'I can't pretend to be overjoyed about any of this,' she said coolly. 'I hope you're not expecting me to attend the wedding?'

'There are only two essential participants,' responded her son with irony. 'Plus the witnesses, of course, but that's already arranged.'

'Good. I only hope it doesn't get into the papers.'

'It's a common enough name. No reason why any connection should be made.'

'I suppose not.' Her tone hardened a fraction more. 'After fifteen years I imagine most will have forgotten there ever was a son!'

'It's more than possible.' Ty sounded unmoved by the implied accusation. 'Adam made an adequate substitute.'

'He isn't family.'

'He's been married to Teresa for sixteen years. How long does it take?'

Denise Morgan's expression was frosty. 'You know very well what I mean. You should be sitting where Adam is sitting right now. Just because you couldn't always see eye to eye with your father ...'

'We were from different planets,' interrupted Ty harshly. 'And I'm not going into all that again. I'm not interested in the business. I never was.'

'And what about me?'

'Your shares are safe enough in Adam's hands. Whatever else you might think of him, he can handle the company.' He stood up abruptly and moved across to the nearest window, sticking his hands in his trouser-pockets as he gazed out on to sunlit lawns. 'I'd have gone crazy,' he observed, almost to himself. 'I still would.'

'I was hardly suggesting a takeover bid,' retorted his mother on a caustic note. 'You left it a little too late for that.' Her eyes met Ria's, expression unchanged. 'At least you'll have some idea of the kind of life you'll be leading, although I can't say I approve of subjecting a child to it. Still, that's your affair. When are you planning on leaving?'

'I—I'm not sure.' Ria shot a desperate glance in Ty's direction, willing him to turn round and scotch the whole idea. She and Steven weren't going anywhere, and that was certain. Their life was right here in England. If Ty had other plans then he could think again!

CHAPTER TWELVE

TERESA'S return to the room coincided with the arrival of her husband and sons, effectively putting paid to any immediate discussion. In his early forties, Adam Townend was a forceful character with a lot of personal charm. He and Ty greeted each other casually, with no hint of restraint or awkwardness on either side.

'Quite a shock to find ourselves with a four-year-old nephew we didn't even know existed,' he said frankly to Ria, acknowledging introductions. 'It must have been a real struggle for you these past few years.'

'Not really,' she responded, warming to the sympathy in his manner. 'I had a lot of help from one source and another.'

'Yes, well, it's all in the past now. You've got Ty to take over the responsibilities.'

'We'll share them,' rejoined the latter before Ria could form an answer. The glance briefly crossing hers was devoid of expression. 'Come and meet him, Adam.'

'And tell Simon and Julian to remember he's only half their age,' interjected Teresa as both men started for the door. She pulled a wry face for Ria's benefit. 'They're at that superior stage where they think they know everything. Simon is two years older at twelve, but Julian is as big so there's a lot of rivalry between them.'

'Simon would be better at boarding-school,' commented his grandmother. 'He needs the discipline.'

'I'll never send either of them away to school.' Teresa had the air of repeating a much-used statement. 'I'd miss them too much.' Her smile appealed for Ria's support. 'You'd hate to be without Steven, wouldn't you?'

'Yes,' Ria declared, 'I would.'

'It's something you're going to have to face before too long if he's to have anything of an education at all,' advised Denise Morgan. 'Let's hope he won't waste it the way his father did. That trust was the worst thing that could have happened to him.'

'His godfather left him a lot of money,' explained Teresa, seeing Ria's blank look. 'Part to come when he was twenty-one, the rest when he reached thirty-five. Obviously he never told you about it?'

Ria shook her head, her smile faint. 'We didn't get round to discussing finances.'

'My son is a very wealthy man.' Denise sounded sceptical. 'You must have realised that.'

'I know he's bought a larger boat since I last saw him, that's all.'

The laugh was short. 'My dear, he could afford to buy a whole fleet if he felt like it! Certainly he could provide you with a proper home.'

Unlikely, Ria thought with bitterness. Ty did as he wanted; everyone else fell into line. Only not this time.

It took an effort on her part to get through the rest of the day, to smile and look as if everything in the garden was lovely when inside she was seething with righteous anger and .hurt. Ty had deceived her, not in what he had said but in what he had deliberately refrained from saying. There had never been any intention on his part of making a home here in England. He had confidently anticipated her total agreement to his plans for their future together. Steven aside, she still wouldn't have contemplated a return to the South China seas. (Steven aside, came the unwilling thought, she wouldn't have had the chance.) Her child wasn't going to waste his life messing around in boats!

She refused an invitation to stay on for dinner on the grounds that Steven was already going to be late to bed. Worn out, though happy enough, he was asleep on the rear seat before the car had turned out of the drive.

'He's going to be tired for playgroup in the morning,'

commented Ria, temporarily sidetracked as she glanced back at the small , curled-up figure.

'So don't send him,' said Ty reasonably. 'He can stay with me. It isn't going to be for all that much longer, anyway.'

She was silent for a long moment, looking ahead through the windscreen along the beam of the headlights. 'Did it ever occur to you,' she said at length on a controlled note, 'that I might not be willing to just fall in with your plans?'

'No,' he said evenly. 'You knew my circumstances. What did you expect?'

'Honesty,' she retorted. 'And don't give me that about circumstances. I know them all!'

His mouth twisted. 'My mother, I suppose?'

'As a matter of fact, it was Teresa who told me about the trust.' Ria paused, trying to stay cool and in command. 'Why didn't you tell me yourself?'

'Maybe because I didn't want to be married for my money.'

She drew in a sharp breath. 'If that's what you really believe . . .'

'It isn't what I believe.' He sounded suddenly weary. 'It just seemed irrelevant, that's all. You already knew I wasn't on my uppers. What difference does it make?'

'The difference that you don't have to rely on selling the ship in order to realise capital to start some kind of business over here,' she said. 'We could have a proper home, for one thing.'

'I couldn't live in a house. Not in this country, at any rate.'

Her intake of breath was slower, more measured this time. 'And I couldn't live the way you live.'

'You did once.'

'I was another person then.'

'And some.' The taunt was designed to hurt. 'The girl I knew had more guts in her little finger than you've got in your whole body!'

'The girl you knew didn't have any responsibilities,'

she flashed back. 'She didn't have much sense either, getting mixed up with you in the first place!'

'We can take that as read,' he said. 'It doesn't alter a thing. Steven is my responsibility just as much as yours. I'm not exactly planning on taking you away from civilisation altogether. The skipper's quarters aboard the *Catalina* will stretch to three without any trouble at all. Later we can look for a place on land, maybe even build to our own design.'

'What about Steven's schooling?' she demanded. 'He's due to start the real thing after Christmas.'

'You can teach him the basics yourself with the help of correspondence courses. Plenty of others do it successfully enough.'

'Except that I don't happen to see it as a satisfactory alternative. I'm not a qualified teacher.'

'You wouldn't need to be. How do you think kids in the Australian outback cope?'

'The way they have to. Steven doesn't have to.'

It was a few seconds before he spoke again. His face looked austere in the darkness. 'Do I take it you're having a change of heart?'

'Of mind,' she corrected. 'Hearts don't enter into it, do they?' It was a statement not a question. 'You lied to me, Ty. By omission if nothing else. I suppose you thought that once we were married I'd feel obliged.'

'For God's sake!' He was coldly, furiously angry, yet keeping his voice down in order not to waken the sleeping child. 'I made the position clear enough. My life is out there.'

'And ours is here.'

'No,' he denied. 'Not in the same sense. All you'd be giving up is a dead-end job and a flat you don't even own.'

'Plus my son's future.'

'He'd gain more than he'd lose.'

'I doubt it.' Her voice was ragged. 'Anyway, we're not going to find out. It's over, Ty. You go your way and I'll go mine. I was a fool to think it could ever work out.'

He seemed about to say something else, then apparently thought better of it, clamping his mouth tight. The atmosphere settled over them like a pall. Ria could scarcely see through the film over her eyes. Finished before it had even begun. Some epitaph! It was going to be hard picking up the pieces again yet she had no choice. Ty asked too much.

No further word passed between them during the rest of the journey. Only when they drew up before the house did Ty say roughly, 'We have to talk this through.'

'There's nothing to discuss,' she said with finality. 'You have your viewpoint and I have mine. We're neither of us going to give way, so what's the use of talking?'

His breath hissed between clenched teeth. 'You really think I'm just going to leave it at that?'

There was a total lack of emotion in the lift of her shoulders. 'You know the alternative.'

'That isn't an alternative, it's an ultimatum. Did you stop to consider Steven's interests at all?'

'He's the one I am considering.'

'No, you're not. You don't want to share him, that's the real problem. It doesn't matter to you that he's going to be the one missing out.'

'He managed for four years without a father,' she said on the same flat intonation. 'He'll soon forget you again—the same way I will.'

'Just like that?' He reached out for her suddenly, dragging her round with a hard hand. His face was grim in the lamplight, eyes glittering. 'We'll see how easy you'll find it!'

Ria held herself rigid against the bruising kiss, rejecting her own stirring emotions. She had got by without him before; she could do it again. No way was he going to use sex as a lever.

'You're a hard little bitch,' he grated when he finally let her go. 'O.K., if that's the way you want it, I'll fight you for him!'

She was trembling deep down inside but her voice was steady enough. 'There's no court in the country would grant you custody under the circumstances, so don't waste your time.'

'We'll see,' he said again. 'Right now he should be in bed.'

'You can carry him as far as the door,' she responded, 'but no further. I can manage on my own from there.'

The strong mouth twisted. 'Don't worry, I'm not going to force my way in.'

Getting out of the car, Ria felt the weakness in her limbs, like a creeping paralysis. A core of desperation was beginning to form, tightening her chest until she could scarcely breathe. She wanted to say something—anything that might stop this terrible charade—but no words would break through the barriers.

Somehow she managed to make her way up the short path ahead of Ty with his burden. Steven, thank heaven, hadn't even stirred. With the door opened at last, she turned and held out her arms, meeting the cold grey eyes with difficulty.

'All right, I'll take him.'

Ty handed over the sleeping child without protest, turning at once and striding off down the path. Ria didn't wait to see him get back in the car, closing the door with a push of her hip and making for the stairs. She heard the engine spring to life as her foot found the fourth tread, fading away into the distance until all was quiet again.

The numbness lasted all the way through getting Steven undressed and into his bed. Only when the covers were tucked in around the small, dead-to-the-world figure and she was free to go through to the lonely living-room did it begin to lift. In the space of a few hours her life had changed all over again. She and Ty were alienated now—on opposite sides of the fence. The threat to fight her for custody had been merely that, of course. He was far from being fool enough to believe he might stand a chance of winning. Yet she could scarcely credit he would give up this easily either. Steven meant a lot to him. Far more than she ever could.

And that was the crux of the matter, wasn't it? she acknowledged with sudden insight. She was jealous not only of Steven's feelings for his father, but of Ty's for his son too. What kind of a person did that make her?

Sleep came fitfully that night. Up at six-thirty, Ria viewed her lacklustre eyes in the bathroom mirror and wondered how she was going to get through the coming week. Wednesday should have been her wedding day. Perhaps not the kind most women dreamed of, but real enough for all of it. It still wasn't too late. If she rang Ty now and told him she had changed her mind he would take it from there. Except that she hadn't changed her mind, had she? Leaving emotion aside, the same problems applied.

Steven had to be woken for once. Tousle-headed and sleepy-eyed, he was so dear she simply had to hold him, hugging him to her until he complained she was squashing him.

'Where's Daddy?' he asked over breakfast. 'Didn't he stay last night?'

'He couldn't,' she said, hurting inside at what she was doing. 'He . . . had to go away again.'

Grey-blue eyes filled suddenly with tears. 'I don't want him to go away.'

'It won't be for long.' Better, Ria thought, to allow the memory to fade over time than to tell the truth now. She added on a bright note, 'You'll be going to school four mornings this week, like we said. That will make the time go faster.'

He cheered up a little at the thought. School was fun. 'I'll draw Daddy a picture of his ship,' he announced. 'An' I'll colour it with my crayons.'

She said softly, 'When did he tell you about his ship?'

'One night after he read me my story. He said it was big and black with three masts and a funnel. I expect he's gone to get it ready for us all, like he said. Won't it be exciting living on a ship, Mummy?'

'Yes.' There was little else she could say. He'd forget about it eventually. Children had notoriously short memories. He might miss Ty for a little while, but he'd get over that too in the end. He hadn't known his father long enough to form any real attachment.

Margaret was waiting downstairs as usual to take over her charge. Having gone back for a handkerchief, Ria was a couple of minutes after her son in reaching the lower regions. One look at the older woman's face was enough to tell her that the news was out.

'I sent him out to the back to find Clancy,' said the other. 'What's all this about Ty leaving again? I thought the wedding was supposed to be this week?'

'There isn't going to be any wedding.' Ria tried to say it matter-of-factly. 'I made a mistake thinking we could make a go of it after all this time.'

Margaret studied her shrewdly. 'What did he do wrong?'

'It's not so much a case of what he did but of what he expected.' Ria paused, conscious of a certain reticence. 'He took it for granted we'd both be going back East with him.'

'Understandable, I suppose, if that's where he's made his home.'

'He lives on board his ship. You think that's a suitable home for a small boy?'

'Depends how big it is. I knew a family from round the corner who sold up and bought a sailing yacht and took off round the world a few years ago. Finished up in New Zealand.'

'It's hardly the same thing. With Ty it's a business.'

'With most sailors it's a way of life. My brother was a merchant seaman—never really happy to be on dry land. You can hardly expect him to give it up just like that.'

'Why not?' Ria's tone was brusque. 'He expects me to give up my way of life.'

Margaret lifted her eyebrows. 'So what's so wonderful about the way you live? You could have married Keith months ago if this was all you wanted. You're twenty-five, girl, not forty. You need to get out and start enjoying yourself before it's too late.'

'At Steven's expense.'

The snort was derisive. 'Don't use him as an excuse. You're the one who got cold feet. What is it, too much man for you?'

Ria was staring at her with startled eyes. 'I didn't realise you liked him all that much.'

'It took me a day or two to come round, but he has a way with him all right. He's what you need—what you both need. Somebody who'll take good care of you and give you all the things you've been missing.' She paused, tone altering a fraction. 'If you'll take my advice, you'll get on that phone right now and tell him you've had time to think things over.'

'I don't think so.' Ria's throat hurt, but she was resolute. 'It's best this way.'

'Yes, well, I hope you'll be able to convince Steven of that when he's old enough to realise what you robbed him of.'

Ria made a show of glancing at her watch. 'I'm going to miss my bus if I don't look slippy. Say goodbye to Steven for me. I'll be home at the usual time.'

It was a relief to be out of the house and walking in the clear, chill air. Margaret's stance might have taken her aback for a moment or two but it hadn't altered anything. Both Margaret and Ty were wrong—it was essential to keep on believing that.

The day was long, every ring of the telephone a jerk at her heartstrings. Common sense told her Ty would be unlikely to ring the office where every word she said could be overheard, only it didn't make any difference to her nerve responses. She could only be thankful that she had told no one about the wedding, having intended to make the announcement after it was accomplished fact. She knew curiosity still ran rife where members of the staff were concerned, and told herself it could continue to do so. Eventually the whole topic would die a natural death.

Tuesday was worse because there had been the faint hope at the back of her mind that Ty might put in an appearance at the house the previous night with some kind of compromise to offer. His failure to contact her in any way at all suggested a possible withdrawal from the fray on his part—perhaps because he had realised the futility in attempting to carry out his threat. There was every chance that she might never see him again, yet she wouldn't allow herself to care. Caring hurt too much.

The personal call came in around twelve thirty, drawing her to the phone with fast-beating heart and a curt little speech all prepared. Margaret's voice came as a shock, all the more so because she sounded so agitated.

'I got held up and was late going to pick Steven up from playgroup,' she said, running the words into each other in her haste to explain. 'Only he'd already gone. They said his father had fetched him just after ten-thirty. I told them they shouldn't have let him go like that, only it was a new teacher and she didn't realise there was anything unusual. I'm sorry, Ria. I should have been there earlier. I don't know what to do. Do you think he might have taken the little mite home with him?'

If by home she meant his mother's apartment, Ria doubted it. Both mind and limbs felt frozen. Steven would come to no harm with his father, for certain, only that was little comfort right now. Parental abduction was nothing new; it happened all the time. By now they could be anywhere. If this was his way of convincing her that he meant business then he was going the wrong way about it. The police would see it in quite another light.

'Ria?' Margaret sounded distraught. 'Are you all right?'

'Yes, of course.' The words were automatic, her mind clicking back into action. 'I'll meet you at home. Just wait until I get there.'

Colin looked at her with concern when she replaced the receiver. 'Something wrong? You're as white as a sheet.'

'I have to go home,' she said. 'Steven ... he's gone missing.'

'Oh, God, I'm sorry! Anything I can do?'

She shook her head, summoning a smile. 'I don't suppose it's all that serious. If you'd just let Mr Hardy know when he gets back from lunch.'

'Yes, sure.'

He had passed the news around by the time she came out from the cloakroom dressed for outdoors, but she didn't linger for any words of sympathy. At this hour of the day the journey home took only half the normal time. She made it with the faint hope in her heart that Ty would have had second thoughts and brought the boy back home by the time she got there—a hope she knew to be futile the moment she saw Margaret's face.

'There's a letter and a couple of packets for you,' she said, pointing to the hall table. 'Came in the second post. I thought one of them might be from Ty.'

The letter was. Posted the previous evening, it was short and wholly to the point.

> Considering all the angles, [he had written] it seems there's only one way to make you see sense and that's to take matters out of your hands. By the time you read this we'll be on a plane heading east. If you want to see Steven again you'll have to follow. There's a ticket in your name in the post. All you have to do is use it.

It was easier simply to pass the letter over for Margaret to read for herself than to relate the contents. Ria felt oddly unemotional, as if she had known all along what Ty had intended. She slit the larger of the two slim packets, taking out the enclosed air ticket and opening it at the first page. Heathrow to Brunei direct.

The plane would put down at Singapore, of course, and probably in a couple of other place before that, but she would be going straight through. She had to go. Ty had left her with no choice in the matter. But she wouldn't be staying, that was for sure.

The other packet contained a couple of copies of the photograph they had had taken in Trafalgar Square. Ty was holding Steven on his shoulders with one hand, the other arm curved about her own. They looked so happy, she thought achingly: a real family. Not even a week ago yet, and look where they were now.

'What are you going to do?' asked Margaret as she continued to stand there looking at the photograph.

'I'll be on the first available flight, of course,' Ria said, still without looking up. 'And home again on the next one out.'

'That's going to cost. What if he won't provide the funds?'

'Then I'll go to the Brunei police and tell them the whole story. They're fond of children over there. They'll see the right thing gets done.'

'Always providing they see it the same way you do.' Margaret hesitated. 'I can lend you a few hundred if it will help.'

'Thanks.' There was gratitude in Ria's smile. 'I might just take you up on that.'

'What about work?'

'I'll have to ask for leave of absence.' Her mind was already jumping ahead, calculating what needed to be done. 'I can check seat availability now, then I'll at least have something to work to. I'll need to take some clothes for Steven.'

'I daresay his father will have provided for that.'

Ria paused with a foot on the lower tread of the stairs, looking back at her landlady and friend with darkened blue eyes. 'I don't want anything from Ty Morgan except my son!'

Landing formalities at Bandar Seri Bagawan's modern

air terminal were surprisingly swift and smooth. Breathing in the humid heat as she waited for a taxi to take her to the deep water port at Maura seventeen miles away, Ria could almost imagine that the last five years had never been. The changes were in her, not in her surroundings. She had been a girl then, she was a woman now—and a mother.

The three days since Ty had taken her son away had seemed like a lifetime. He was cruel and heartless and any feeling she might have had for the man had long since vanished. She was staying only as long as it took her to arrange transport back home to England. Let him try to stop her at his peril. Margaret had put up the funds for two return tickets. It was going to take a long time to pay her back but the other had stated she was in no hurry for the money. At the very least it gave her independence.

It had been late afternoon when she had landed and darkness had fallen long before she reached her destination. The taxi driver asked for the location of the *Catalina* at the dock gates, then drove her the whole distance along the wharf to stop at length beside a ship three times the size of the old *Tiger Rose*. Ria added a substantial tip for the man's cheerful services, refusing his offer to carry her suitcase up the gangway on the grounds that it wasn't heavy enough to warrant assistance.

She could see signs of movement above as she started up the metal treads. A man wearing denims and a dark jersey loomed over her the moment she reached the head of the gangway, effectively blocking any further progress.

'You the one we're expecting?' he asked in strong Australian accents.

'I'm Ria Brownlow,' she said. 'Is my son on board?'

'Young Steve?' White teeth flashed in a grin. 'Yeah, he's here. They're waiting for you in the skipper's cabin.' He held out a hand for the suitcase. 'Carry your bag?'

'How is it I was expected today?' asked Ria, falling into step at his side along the deck. 'I didn't notify anyone I was going to be on that flight.'

'Guess the skipper checked the passenger list. Any rate, he was definite enought.' He slanted a glance, taking in the smart, lightweight trouser suit and smoothly brushed fair hair. 'Not your first time in Brunei, I understand. Notice any changes on the way through?'

'Not to mention.' Ria wondered just how much he did know. Had Ty made free with the whole affair?

'I'm the first mate, by the way,' added her companion, yanking open a watertight door. 'Drew Baxter by name. Been with the *Catalina* since the skipper took her over a couple of years back. It's a good berth. Best I've had.' He stopped and rapped his knuckles against one of the inner doors set along the short alleyway, opening it and sticking his head through to announce informally, 'She's here, skipper. Safe and sound!'

Ria stepped past him into the cabin, to be greeted by a whirlwind as Steven flung himself into her arms.

'Where've you been all this time?' he demanded, hugging her fiercely as she held him. 'Why didn't you come straight away? We've waited and waited!'

Blue eyes met grey over the top of the dark head, the latter unflinching in their regard. 'She's here now,' said Ty. 'That's all that matters.'

The mate had left her suitcase on the floor just inside the door and withdrawn, leaving the three of them alone. Still clutching her son, Ria took a grip on her emotions. 'It won't be for long,' she said. 'There's a flight out on Monday.'

'You don't waste much time.' Ty's mouth was sardonic. 'At least sit down and get your breath. I daresay there's plenty you want to tell me.'

'You can count on it.' With the first flush of enthusiasm over, Steven was already wriggling to get down. She lowered him gently to the floor, keeping an arm across his shoulders in a gesture as much possessive as protective. 'If you were so sure I was going to be coming today, you could have been at the airport to meet me.'

'I thought you'd prefer a less public confrontation,' he responded evenly. 'Anyway, we can discuss the pros and cons later. Hungry?'

Ria shook her head. 'I ate on the plane.'

'That had to be tea. I'm talking about a proper meal.'

'I'm not hungry!' She caught herself up as Steven lifted his face to her, summoning a smile. 'Just a bit tired after so many hours travelling, that's all. We were held up at Singapore.'

'Sounds about par for the course.' He was on his feet, big and powerful in the denims and T-shirt. Memory stirred in her; it took a conscious effort to hold back the past. This man had stolen her child. She had to keep her mind on that fact. Once she got away from here she didn't care if she never saw him again.

'I wouldn't say no to some coffee,' she said into the pause.

'I'll get it.' He was moving as he spoke, lips twisting as she stepped aside to give him room to pass. 'There's a mini-galley at the back of the bridge so it won't take long. Make yourself at home.'

She felt the tension in her relax a little as he went out. Steven tugged at her jacket.

'Come and see the drawings I've done!'

A small table set between two banquette seats against the far bulkhead held paper and crayons scattered in the hasty departure on her arrival. Ria helped straighten things out, duly admiring the wavy but instantly recognisable outlines of the ship with its matchstick crew members. The cabin itself was large and comfortable, furnished for daytime use. A cardboard box beneath the table held several toys of the kind designed to appeal to a small boy.

'Were you afraid coming all this way on your own?' she asked as her son bent his head once more to his drawing, tongue protruding a little with the effort of concentration.

'I wasn't on my own,' he said without looking up. 'Daddy was with me. He said you'd be coming along the next day, only you didn't.'

'I got on the first plane I could,' she defended.

'It doesn't matter now, Mummy,' he assured her kindly. 'Isn't it a smashing ship? Daddy's the captain, did you know?'

Her heart ached at the pride in that statement. 'Yes, I know. What else have you been doing since you got here?'

'Oh, lots of things.' He changed crayons, choosing a vivid blue to represent the sea. 'We saw some houses sticking out of the water with lots of little bridges in between, and some people doing karate dancing.' He pronounced the word without stumbling. 'Daddy says they only do it on special occasions. Did you ever see them when you were here before I was born?'

'No,' she was bound to confess.

'Well, I suppose you will now.'

Ty came back with the coffee before she could find an adequate reply. He had brought two mugs.

'We don't run to cups and saucers,' he said, handing one over. Grey eyes challenged her. 'What this ship needs is a woman's touch.'

Not this woman, she thought, but refrained from saying it out loud. Getting Steven away from his father was going to be difficult enough without making an issue of every taunt.

'I don't have a hotel booked,' she said. 'Perhaps . . .'

'No problem. You can have my cabin, I'll sleep in here.' The smile was slow. 'Quite like old times. Steve has his own berth. Which reminds me, old son, it's about time you were hitting the sack. Clear your things up first, though.'

Ria sat sipping her coffee while her son carried out instructions. She didn't like the thought of letting him out from under her eye again, yet the sooner he was in

bed the sooner she could begin to make the position
totally clear where Ty was concerned. A few days more
and they would be away. Nothing or no one was going
to stop her.

She saw Steven into bed herself, impressed by his
knowhow as he manipulated the shower set into a
cubicle next to the head. His pyjamas were of the finest
cotton in a pale blue that went with his eyes. Dressed in
them, with skin glowing, he brought a lump to her
throat. Already, after three short days, he was acquiring
a healthy tan, emphasised by the paler line where
diminutive bathing trunks had been. Daddy had been
pleased to find he could swim so well, he told her
proudly. They had been twice to the beach.

Ty's cabin was next door. Ria took a swift look in
before returning to where he waited for her. There
were two berths, one above the other, and ample
storage facilities. Not that it concerned her, she
hastened to assure herself. She was hardly going to be
here long enough to unpack, much less put anything
away.

He was talking on the intercom when she returned to
the main cabin, switching off on her entry.

'O.K.?' he asked.

'Fine.' She stifled a yawn, feeling the weariness of the
long flight catching up with her. There were too many
things that needed thrashing out to give in to bodily
needs as yet. 'You seem to have packed a lot into three
days from what he was telling me.'

He shrugged lightly. 'It took my mind off the port
charges I've been paying here while we waited—to say
nothing of the cargoes I've lost.'

'You can afford it.' She refused to entertain
sympathy. 'If you want to load up tomorrow I'll be
more than willing to find accommodation ashore over
the weekend.'

'I can stand a few more days,' he came back on a dry
note. 'Why don't you give in and get some rest? You
look thoroughly jet-lagged.'

'That's a comfort.' She shook her head. 'There are things we have to talk about first.'

'Such as what? According to what you were saying earlier, your mind is already made up. I'm not going to try arguing you into changing it.'

Ria eyed him suspiciously. 'You mean you're just going to let us leave?'

'Isn't that what you want?'

'Yes.' Her tone gained emphasis. 'Yes, of course it is.'

'So go and get some sleep. There's the whole weekend to get through.'

It would be stupid not to comply, Ria acknowledged. She was both physically and mentally below par. Her shoulders lifted in rueful acceptance. 'I suppose you're right. I haven't had much sleep at all since all this happened.'

'I'll make my apologies in the morning when we're both in a fit state of mind,' he stated briefly. 'I'm going ashore, so you'll not be disturbed.'

To find comfort in some lady-friend's arms, no doubt, came the caustic thought, rooting out any small seeds of forgiveness.

She was too tired to do anything much beyond undressing and getting into night attire. There would be time enough in the morning to shower and wash her hair. Time enough for everything.

Lying there in the lower berth, she let herself drift, not thinking of anything beyond the comfort of the mattress and the growing heaviness of her limbs. Vague sounds came from all parts of the ship: the creaking and groaning of metal plate, the occasional thud or clang; the faint, faraway calling of voices dissolving slowly into her dreams.

She was back in the locker aboard the *Tiger Rose* just before she awoke again, feeling the rise and fall of the sea beneath her. Someone was shaking her.

'Mummy, we're sailing. The ship's sailing!' Steven was beside himself with excitement, small face lit from within. 'There's no land any more!'

Awareness came swiftly as the mists cleared. Not the
Tiger Rose but the *Catalina*. Not night any more but
broad daylight. Throwing back the single sheet, Ria slid
from the berth and crossed to the port, staring out at
the sunlit seascape with eyes growing stormier by the
second. Steven was right, there was no sign of land.
How long they had been at sea she had no way of
knowing for certain, but it had to be several hours. Ty
had tricked her, persuading her to retire to bed so he
could get the ship under way while she slept. Tired as
she had been, he must have realised she was unlikely to
waken to the movement.

Steven was already dressed in the same shorts and shirt
he had worn the previous night, his feet bare. There was
no carpet on the floor, just a couple of rattan mats.

'Go and put your sandals on,' she instructed
automatically. 'And wait for me before you try going
up on deck.'

'Daddy will be on the bridge,' he said with an air of
experience. 'That's where the captain drives the ship.'

'Steers,' she corrected, reaching for her things. 'You
can take me up there just as soon as I'm dressed if you
know the way.'

'I know where everything is. Daddy showed me.'

Daddy said, Daddy did—Ria clenched her teeth
against the need to hit out at something. Daddy was
going to turn right round and take them back to the
dock if he knew what was good for him. Whatever he
had in mind, it wasn't going to work.

A quick splash of water over her face was all she
allowed herself for the present; the shower could come
later. With her face free of make-up and her hair still
tumbled, she allowed Steven to lead her along the alley
and up the short companionway which gave access to
the roomy control deck. Ty was talking to the mate;
another man was at the helm. The latter took little
notice of the newcomers, his attention fully occupied by
the task in hand. Drew Baxter looked wary and
uncomfortable as he caught Ria's eye.

'Morning,' he proffered. 'There's some fresh coffee if you'd like it?'

She shook her head, gaze on the man behind him. 'Ty, I want to talk to you. Alone, if you don't mind.'

Face unrevealing, he nodded to the younger man. 'Take Steve out on deck for a few minutes, will you, Drew.' To the helmsman he added, 'I'll take over.'

Ria waited until they had the bridge to themselves before letting fly, her voice cracking with sheer pent-up emotion. 'I don't know what you thought this was going to achieve, but . . .'

'Time,' he said succinctly. 'I'm buying time.'

'For what?'

'To persuade you.'

Her breath felt trapped in her throat. 'You won't succeed,' she forced out.

He had his back to her, his feet planted slightly apart for balance in the way she remembered so well. His hips were just as lean in the form-fitting denims, his legs so long and strong. She could feel her defences crumbling even before he spoke.

'I haven't even started trying yet. We're going to Sibu. Jemo and Rahim will be there to meet us when we dock. I didn't think it wise to try taking Steve any further up river until his shots have had time to take.'

'You've had him inoculated?' she demanded, momentarily distracted.

'Of course I've had him inoculated. Took it like a trooper. He had a sore arm for a few hours, that's all. He'll get his second dose in a couple of weeks, then he'll be in the clear.'

'He won't be here in a couple of weeks.' Ria tried to make her tone firm. 'I realise I can't force you to turn back to Brunei, but I can, and shall, leave the ship the minute we dock at Sibu.'

'If you still want to by then I'll deserve it,' he said. 'Why don't you come and take a turn at the wheel? She handles well.'

'We played that scene a long time ago,' she

retorted, stifling the pang. 'I'm not quite so gullible these days.'

'You were irresistible.' His tone was reminiscent. 'I'd never wanted anyone or anything more than I wanted you right then!'

'You had me,' she reminded him. 'That very same night.'

He turned his head to look at her, eyes fired with the memory. 'How could I forget? You told me you loved me.'

'Like the silly little fool I was.' Her voice caught. 'It's hard to believe I could have been quite that naïve!'

'You hadn't learned to hold back then. You said what you thought, what you felt.'

'What I thought I felt. You said it yourself—just infatuation. You were my first experience.'

'Your only experience. That's the way it's going to stay, Ria. If I have to keep us at sea a month to stop you from leaving, I'll do that too. I can't lose you again.'

'Me,' she whispered after a moment, 'or Steven?'

'Both of you. I could have stayed in England, yes, but it wouldn't have worked out. Sooner or later it would have started to come between us. I know myself too well. I can't take any kind of confinement. At the same time, I couldn't give you up, hence the desperate measures.' He paused, mouth wry. 'Don't just stand there. Say something.'

Her smile came slow and just a little shaky. 'Can I change my mind—about that turn at the helm, I mean?'

'Any time.'

There was security within the circle of his arms. Ria leaned her weight into him, the way she had yearned to do that day so many years before, feeling his strength, his hardness—giving emotion free rein at last.

'I think I'm in love with you,' she said softly. 'Have I told you that?'

Ty laughed, bending his head to kiss her temple, then her ear. 'Not often enough!'

Ahead, through the screens, she could see the sky, clear and blue at the moment, but liable to swift change as the monsoon got into its stride. Her feelings wouldn't change, she knew that in her heart. Her love for this man could weather any storm. Steven wouldn't suffer. Not with two of them to care. They were a family now.

New This spring
Harlequin Category Romance Specials!
New Mix

4 Regencies—for more wit, tradition, etiquette ... and romance

2 Gothics—for more suspense, drama, adventure ... and romance

Regencies

A Hint of Scandal by Alberta Sinclair
She was forced to accept his offer of marriage, but could she live with her decision?

The Primrose Path by Jean Reece
She was determined to ruin his reputation and came close to destroying her own!

Dame Fortune's Fancy by Phyllis Taylor Pianka
She knew her dream of love could not survive the barrier of his family tradition....

The Winter Picnic by Dixie McKeone
All the signs indicated they were a mismatched couple, yet she could not ignore her heart's request....

Gothics

Mirage on the Amazon by Mary Kistler
Her sense of foreboding did not prepare her for what lay in waiting at journey's end....

Island of Mystery by Margaret M. Scariano
It was the perfect summer job, or so she thought—until it became a nightmare of danger and intrigue.

Don't miss any of them!

Take
4 novels and a surprise gift
FREE

ATTRACTIVE, SPACE SAVING BOOK RACK

Display your most prized novels on this handsome and sturdy book rack. The hand-rubbed walnut finish will blend into your library decor with quiet elegance, providing a practical organizer for your favorite hard-or soft-covered books.

Only $9.95

Approximately 16" x 8" when assembled

Assembles in seconds!

To order, rush your name, address and zip code, along with a check or money order for $10.70* ($9.95 plus 75¢ postage and handling) payable to *Harlequin Reader Service*:

Harlequin Reader Service
Book Rack Offer
901 Fuhrmann Blvd.
P.O. Box 1325
Buffalo, NY 14269-1325

Offer not available in Canada.

*New York residents add appropriate sales tax.

BKR-1R

Harlequin Presents

Coming Next Month

975   DARK ENCHANTMENT   Helen Bianchin
A young Australian's feelings for the man she's to marry veer crazily
between attraction and resentment. The match would cement a
financial empire. Love—for him anyway—seems entirely incidental.

976   A WILLING SURRENDER   Robyn Donald
It's love versus family loyalty for an au-pair girl who falls in love with the
man who broke up her brother's marriage. Her head urges caution. But
her heart cries out "Surrender."

977   AN IDEAL MATCH   Sandra Field
They might be the perfect match—a music teacher who can't have
children and a widowed professor with three of his own. The attraction is
there. So why does he warn her not to fall in love with him?

978   DESIRE FOR REVENGE   Penny Jordan
Love at first sight.... It all seems possible when a London editor comes
face-to-face with a sapphire-eyed stranger at a masquerade ball. But
fantasy collides with reality when she returns to the real world....

979   A LONG WAY FROM HEAVEN   Susanne McCarthy
A hotel owner in the Grenadines is left in financial arrears when her
husband dies. Her only way out is marriage to a man she once loved—a
man whose pride wanted her, not his heart!

980   BEYOND RANSOM   Sophie Weston
An agronomist in South America is kidnapped by revolutionaries and
forced to pose as the leader's woman for her own safety. But she feels
decidedly unsafe when she no longer has to *pretend* to love him.

981   PASSION'S DAUGHTER   Sara Wood
It's one thing for a Gypsy girl to love the lord of the manor, quite another
to think their marrying would bring happiness—no matter what he says
in the heat of the moment.

982   FANCY FREE   Karen van der Zee
An adventure tour company owner thinks she has it all until she falls for
a dynamic but conservative man. He wants a wife and children, but
seems willing to settle for a long-distance affair in the meantime.

Available in May wherever paperback books are sold, or through
Harlequin Reader Service:

In the U.S.
901 Fuhrmann Blvd.
P.O. Box 1397
Buffalo, N.Y. 14240-1397

In Canada
P.O. Box 603
Fort Erie, Ontario
L2A 5X3